KT-199-451

LINDA ARONSON

A Comedy of Love
and Seaweed

KELP

Born and brought up in London, Linda Aronson joined the Bank of England as a Sub-Assistant Deputy Tea Lady (D sector) and left for Australia shortly after initiating the Great Tea Trolley Nastiness of 1971. She has remained there ever since.

She lives in Sydney with her husband and two children and works as a playwright and screenwriter. *Kelp* is her first novel. Her best known work is *Dinkum Assorted*, possibly the world's only stage musical written for fifteen women and a goat.

Kelp

A comedy of love and seaweed

LINDA ARONSON

MACMILLAN CHILDREN'S BOOKS

First published 1997 by
Pan Macmillan Australia Pty Limited

This edition produced for The Guide Association

First published in the UK 1998 by
Macmillan Children's Books
a division of Macmillan Publishers Limited
25 Eccleston Place, London SW1W 9NF
Basingstoke and Oxford
www.macmillan.com
Associated companies throughout the world

ISBN 0 330 36949 0

Copyright © Linda Aronson 1997

The right of Linda Aronson to be identified as the
author of this work has been asserted by her in accordance
with the Copyright, Designs and Patents Act 1988.

All rights reserved. No part of this publication may be
reproduced, stored in or introduced into a retrieval system,
or transmitted, in any form, or by any means (electronic,
mechanical, photocopying, recording or otherwise) without
the prior written permission of the publisher. Any person
who does any unauthorized act in relation to this
publication may be liable to criminal prosecution and civil
claims for damages.

7 9 8 6

A CIP catalogue record for this book is available
from the British Library.

Printed and bound in Great Britain by
Mackays of Chatham plc, Chatham, Kent

This book is sold subject to the condition that it shall not,
by way of trade or otherwise, be lent, re-sold, hired out,
or otherwise circulated without the publisher's prior consent
in any form of binding or cover other than that in which
it is published and without a similar condition including this
condition being imposed on the subsequent purchaser.

For Lisa, Jack and Mark

Special thanks to Nikki Christer
and Cathy Proctor

SPECIAL ACKNOWLEDGEMENT

Kelp sprang from an idea of my friend—
the writer, film producer and avid cook,
Ken Methold. That it happened as a novel
rather than as a TV comedy series is again
due to Ken, but it also has a lot to do with
a bag of lambs' kidneys.

Ken had an idea for a TV comedy
series. It was about the batty inhabitants
of a Queensland island and he employed
me and another scriptwriter, Morgan
Smith, to write it. Morgan soon dropped
out, but I persisted, fortified not only by
Ken's encouragement and fine comic
sense, but also by his magnificent lunches.

Television companies here and overseas heard of *Kelp*. They were dying to see
the scripts!

Finally, one hot summer morning, Ken
and I set off to meet the TV executives at
their huge and glamorous premises. And

then it happened. Ken saw the butcher's shop and his eyes lit up ...

We walked into the gleaming office building clutching not only the scripts, but a bag of prime Australian lambs' kidneys. We might have got away with it if the air-conditioning hadn't broken down.

As the sun blasted down upon us, Ken and I began to cook. So did the kidneys. By the time the TV executives arrived, the room was filled with the overpowering fragrance of simmering offal. We never heard from the TV company again.

A year or so later, after we had experimented with the idea of *Kelp* as a film, Ken leant over the soup pot and said: 'You should write it as a novel.' So I did. I turned the film version inside out, added three hundred extra seals, created the world of Yarradindi High—and had some of the best fun in my life.

But it never would have happened without Ken and his kidneys.

LINDA ARONSON
23 August 1996

Chapter 1

I close my eyes. Here goes. . .

The white Porsche swings hungrily down the curves of the carpark. Three storeys below, Eddie runs madly to the lift doors. The parking attendant's uniform flatters his lean athletic body and the wind whips his short blond hair. The lift doors slide open as he reaches them. Conchita, the young maid, stares anxiously at him. She holds up the briefcase reverently, unconsciously stroking the monogrammed 'ET'. 'I thought we'd miss her.'

'No way,' Eddie's face breaks into a proud smile. 'Because of us, Emily won't have to go without her briefcase.'

The Porsche screeches up beside them, the engine throbbing. Eddie leaps to its side. The electric window purrs down.

'Ma'am. You forgot this.' Eddie's voice is husky as he hands the briefcase into the fine, manicured fingers that extend from the window.

'Thank you, Eddie.' The voice is deep, warm and feminine—strong yet infinitely mysterious. 'And please, my name is "Emily".'

Eddie swallows hard. 'Yes, Ma'am . . . I mean, Emily.' Conchita instinctively bobs a curtsy. The gleaming car lunges forward and out onto the street. Conchita and Eddy stare yearningly. How many hours until they see her again?

A group of anxious young executives wait restlessly in the boardroom of Emily Enterprises. Emily strides along the corridor, her legs impossibly shapely, her walk long and even atop her shining stiletto heels.

'Emily! I'm talking to you!'

Oh no, it's Tiff! Just as I'm getting to the good part!

She walks into the boardroom. Despite themselves, despite knowing that the woman in front of them has one of the most powerful and brilliant business minds in the world, an involuntary sigh at her sheer overwhelming beauty goes up and hangs in the air like perfume.

'Emily! I told you to get in the washing!'

Now my mum's coming as well! Quick!

One young man holding a single rose steps forward awkwardly.

'Emily, forgive me for being this forward.'

'Yes, Brett,' breathed Emily huskily.

'Emily! What have you let the twins do to themselves? They're covered in mud!'

That's my mum, Blanche. I'm desperately trying to hang on to my daydream because Brett is about to propose to me, but Tiff suddenly says, 'Stevie? What's in your mouth?'

She sticks a finger into Stevie's wet, dribbly little mouth and shrieks, 'Oh my God, he's got a snail in his mouth! Blanche, Stevie's got a snail in his mouth!'

That's it. Gone. My concentration is shattered and the world of Emily Enterprises gives way to reality. Which is, two-year-old Stevie bawling horribly, his twin Jeremy with a rope of snot hanging from one nostril, Tiff my auntie waving a spit-covered snail and Blanche my mum going ballistic about (tick the answer of your choice): my irresponsibility, my day-dreaming, shutting myself up in my room, my dislike of peanut butter sandwiches, etc, etc.

Mum and Tiff have exactly the same legs, bodies, fluffy red hair and look of outrage—except that Blanche won't wear glasses like the rest of us so her look of outrage is aimed at the middle distance rather than my face. More at the chook coop—or jumble of bits of wood, old trellis and chicken wire that count for a chook coop. Tiff is sticking the snail between my eyes and raving on about what damage it could have done to Stevie. Personally, my sympathies are with the snail.

I say, 'Sorry.'

This is their cue to say the word 'sorry' several times—their voices becoming higher each time—then explain in great detail why my apology is completely useless. I wonder why I bother.

It's actually not necessary for me to be

present during all this. So I leave. I shove my glasses back up my nose. I stride off in my unshiny rubber boots on my impossibly horrible legs. I take a short cut through the factory to the beach.

Our family lives on an island off the coast of Victoria. We process seaweed for a living. Our factory looks like something out of one of those horrific, medieval depictions of hell. If hell has a stench, it's the steamy, green, salt-cabbagy smell of kelp.

The factory is dark and the floor is ankle deep in hot, green stuff. There are huge bubbling cauldrons dripping hot, green stuff. There are endless fat pipes (winding around dark walls) dripping hot, green stuff. There are my relatives dripping hot, green stuff.

They also look as if they stepped out of a medieval depiction of hell. Except for the glasses.

I squelch through and out onto the beach, picking my way among the sunbaking seals and the nesting albatrosses. The sea's crashing in, heavy with kelp. If I kept going long enough I'd hit South America. I stick my hands in my pockets. I scream for ten seconds. That's better.

Now to write the letter. The fuss over the snail has finally convinced me. Luckily, I've got stamps. I get out my best notepaper. It's a big decision, but my mind is made up.

Mr Rupert Murdoch
News Limited
United States of America

Dear Mr Murdoch,

You might recall me writing to you a couple of times before. I know you must get a lot of letters from people interested in a business career. I am sure they are always asking you to sponsor them in one enterprise or other. Mr Murdoch, I am not asking for sponsorship. I am asking you to adopt me.

Yours sincerely,

Emily Tate

Tate Island
Victoria
Australia

Chapter 2

Let me explain. I am fourteen, my name is Emily Tate and I do not fit in with my family. When you hear about my family you will understand why.

It all stated with my Great-Great Grandpa Tate. He was a seal hunter. He was so short-sighted he had to come to Australia because it was the only place in the world where the seals were tame enough to wait around for him to get them. And, apart from the occasional stabbing of rocks and breaking of spears, get them he did.

He also got married three times and chased girls in between, with the result that for thirty kilometres inland you can still encounter Tates. They come from every possible race, and even the littlest babies have weak eyesight and powerful specs.

These days the seals are protected and have taken a terrible revenge on Great-Great Grandpa by overrunning the island. They are egged on by flocks of extremely aggro albatrosses. The only seals to survive Great-Great Grandpa were either supersmart, huge or ferocious. Now they've interbred. The result is that the entire seal population is supersmart, huge *and* ferocious. In winter and the mating season the island elderly have to be taken about in wheelbarrows to protect them from attacks.

Nowadays, there are about fifty Tates living on Tate Island and many more on the mainland. Because my grandad owns and runs the factory, I belong to the royal family of Tate Island. This means I get to live in a ramshackle wooden house with lunatics who are even more frightening because they look exactly like me.

Let me give you the picture. We are at dinner, the whole royal family. Me, Grandad, Blanche, Auntie Tiff and Tiff's three children (Cinnamon, Stevie and Jeremy). We are all wearing glasses— except for Blanche—which causes problems because Tiff's cooking has steamed up every glass surface, including those on our faces. The twins' little glasses are held on with elastic. I wonder about the use of the glasses because they're always smeared with gunk. The twins would have to see better with them off than on.

Grandpa hands me a note. It is for Blanche. It reads, 'Pass me the potatoes, you windbag.' I give it to her. She reads it, scribbles on her pad, and hands me a page. It reads, 'Get them yourself, you old goat.' Grandpa has read it even before it reaches him. He growls. He is about to speak. Then he realises that if he does he loses to Blanche. He gets the potatoes himself. He chomps angrily while he thinks of an insult. He writes, 'Lazy nerd'. Nerd? This must be one he's seen on TV. Grandpa's always on the lookout for new insults.

Grandpa and Blanche stopped talking at the dinner table several years ago. I'm not sure exactly which row triggered it. I think it was just the result of being in the family business too long. When you're the only two executives in a family business on an island that is ten minutes by ferry from the nearest mainland, you can argue very easily. There's nothing to curb these arguments, so they reach spectacular proportions over nothing at all. Grandpa once threw a typewriter out of the window because Blanche had insisted that 'sincerely' didn't have a 'c' in it.

They still talk in the office. They couldn't deprive themselves of that pleasure. Talk is simply forbidden at home. Which actually makes things quite peaceful. The result is that Tiff keeps up a monologue of complaints about looking after us all. The only other sounds are the snorts of outrage from Blanche, punctuated by Grandpa's infuriated slurping.

All Tiff's complaints are fair enough, I should add. She *does* do everything around the place. She cleans, she cooks, she does the garden and she brings up her three children (her husband left after the twins were born). You name it, Tiff does it.

But the trouble is, you see, she does it *badly*. Which is a terrible shame because you just can't feel guilty when she moans. In fact you tend to feel really resentful because you have to re-do everything she does, to fix it up.

Tiff makes you a dress—the sleeve unravels as you walk out the door. Tiff cleans the bath—she leaves a huge trail of black gritty gunk leading to the plug-hole. Tiff cooks a roast with an aroma to melt stone—it's still frozen in the middle. So before she's even finished doing anything you're steaming with resentment about how you'll have to put things right again.

It's not all her fault. It's partly the Tate eyesight and having to do things with steamed-up glasses. One day—when I'm rich and famous—I'm having contact lenses. Not just so I can see, but to stop me being identified as a Tate.

Don't get me wrong. I love my family. The problem is that I'm neat, tidy and have a good head for business. And they don't. I love commerce, I can type at sixty words a minute and I'm top of my computer class. While some girls save up for posters of rock stars, I save up to buy business magazines.

Maybe it's my dad's fault that I'm different from the rest of my family. Dad was born into one of the oldest hippie families in Australia. His name is Skye Peacemaker. He dropped out to become a stockbroker. Blanche doesn't talk about him much. Tiff once told me that Blanche

11

woke up one morning to find a note. He wrote that he couldn't stand the pressure and was leaving to find himself in finance.

A few months later I was born. A financial wizard trapped in a Tate body. On Tate Island. Surrounded by Tate seaweed. Even worse, surrounded by Tates. We never hear from my dad. Tiff says he changed his name to Craig something. When I leave school I am going to ring up all the stockbrokers called Craig. When I find my dad, I will threaten to give Blanche his address unless he gets me a job at the stock exchange.

Anyway, things have been building up since I was ten. That was when I realised I could run the factory better than Blanche or Grandpa—particularly after a sea eagle dropped a two-kilo jellyfish on Grandpa's head and he started to think he was back in the war.

Actually, anyone could run the factory better than Grandpa or Blanche. We just have to streamline the operation. And as for selling the stuff . . . ! If we wanted, we could sell our kelp dried, to be used as a thickener in ice-cream, salad dressings, shampoos, toothpastes, textiles—the most amazing things. Or we could sell it as fertiliser. Or we could sell it to the Japanese to use in cooking.

What *do* we sell it for? We boil it up to get out the jelly-producing stuff. Then we sell it exclusively to a little local brewery called Yarradindi Beers to make the froth on their beer stand up.

Yes, I am serious.

We do this because my Great-Great Grandpa fell in love with Mrs Adeline Bogle in 1836. Mrs Adeline Bogle was the wife of William Shakespeare Bogle, who ran Yarradindi Beers. Great-Great Grandpa had to think of some way to keep seeing her, so he started selling them our kelp.

You can get some idea of how cool and street-wise Yarradindi Beers is by their advertising slogan. For the last fifty years it has been, 'If you want a big head, drink Yarradindi Blue.' No comment.

Anyway, my childhood has been ruined by Yarradindi Doug, who is the cartoon character thought up by one of the deeply-unfunny Bogles. Doug appears on all their posters. He is a fat, shiny-faced old man with a big red nose, a glass of frothy beer and an IQ of about ten. There is always a balloon coming out of his mouth reading, 'Now *that's* what I call a fine head!'

The joke is that Yarrandindi Doug's whole world revolves around frothy beer. So, for example, Doug is seen next to a painting of the Mona Lisa. But when he says, 'Now *that's* what I call a fine head!' he's actually referring to—*the head on his beer*. Which I find about as funny as a head-on car collision. Every time I go anywhere someone comes up with a dumb line starting with, 'Now that's what I call a fine ... ' something or other. One day someone will say it and I will personally rip them limb from limb.

Well, I won't, but it helps to pretend. You can cope with a lot by pretending.

So, because my Great-Great Grandpa had a crush on Adeline Bogle over 150 years ago, the rest of us are still cooking kelp for a living.

And because my mum and my grandpa are too pig-headed to listen to anyone— least of all me—nothing is going to change. So you see I am a round peg in a square hole. Or a square peg in a round hole. Either way, my family thinks I'm putting it on. I'm not and I'm sick of it.

I have a daydream every day on my

14

walk to catch the ferry for school. It starts as I leave the house and wave goodbye to the babies. It goes like this. A handsome young investor turns up on the island. (By this time I have waved to a crowd of uncles dragging kelp up the beach.) Then, the handsome young investor installs me as managing director. (By this time I'm past the beach and into the caravan park where lots of my relatives live.)

Now, this is the good bit. Firstly, I renovate the factory completely. (By this time I've waved hello to an army of aunties and patted Fatty, the tame seal.) Then I replace all our ancient equipment. (By now, Clem and Col, my sixty-year-old twin cousins, are giving me soggy biscuits or miniature plastic models of Ronald McDonald.)

By the time I'm at the jetty, I pull off a multimillion-dollar deal with a Japanese company and sell the island. This makes me the youngest self-made, multi-millionaire in the world. (By this time the ferry is looming into sight with Auntie Ruby Tate—who is built like a tank—waving at the helm.)

As we tie up at the wharf on the mainland, the school bus is pulling in and I'm being handed a top business award in

New York. I need this fantasy triumph because at this point Grandpa is usually chugging past in his motor boat with a sign that reads, 'I am being kept a prisoner on this island.'

The bus cheers. Let me die. I sniff my blazer for kelp.

Chapter 3

School's bearable because of my best friend, Vince. He's also a Tate, a cousin from the Koori branch. His dad's a solicitor who'd probably be rich if he wasn't emotionally blackmailed to do all the family's legal work for free. Vince is in my class. We've got a bond developed after years of jokes about kelp and inbreeding and Yarradindi Doug. He keeps me a seat on the bus.

Vince is sitting near the back, as usual. And as usual, the Cool set is sitting near the front to intimidate the driver. Their dreadlocks are like the frizzy, mud-coloured tails my dolly Belinda had after I shampooed her. They have rings in every conceivable place. Plus a few in places it hurts me even to think of. I squeeze past them and I wait for the cracks about kelp and Yarradindi Doug. Five, four, three, two, one . . .

'Hey, Em'ly!'

Right on cue, it's Justin, chief Cool. Justin was a thug even in kindergarten. He destroyed people's Lego and ripped the front page off the Big Bird spelling book.

'Now *that's* what I call a . . . total dork . . .!' he says, and all the Cools snigger.

Vince tosses his eyes towards heaven and shifts his bag for me. As I sit down, I sigh. Why do Cools never laugh? I mean, they *do* laugh, but not at normal things. It's always a kind of protest at the stupidity of others. I suppose on Planet Cool nobody would laugh at all. They'd all slouch around listening to heavy metal and twiddling their nose rings.

This morning the bus is particularly noisy because we have a new bus driver. He doesn't know which bus stops he is supposed to stop at to collect passengers. Foolishly, he asks for advice. This is a bad move.

We sail past our normal stops. Everyone cheers. The bus is starting and stopping and screeching to a halt and reversing. The bus driver is swearing and people are hanging out of the windows. At the shopping centre, next to the billboard of Yarradindi Doug standing next to Marilyn Monroe and preferring his beer, an old man bangs on the door to tell us off. He has a bald head and shorts that come up to his chest. He calls the bus driver a nincompoop and shakes his fist at Justin. Everyone boos.

We get to school early because we go by the new freeway. Nobody tells the driver he's not supposed to go by the freeway because there are another ten kids waiting for him on the back roads.

In Social Studies everyone is passing notes about the school dance. I hate the school dance—Tiff always makes me these hideous outfits. As usual, Justin and the Cools of the class are trying to make our Social Studies teacher, Mrs Mills, get angry. They are trying to get her so angry that she bangs with both hands on her desk.

This is not because they particularly want to get her angry. It's because apparently two years ago she banged her hands like that and her boobs popped out of the front of her dress.

We are doing eco-tourism and talking

19

about 'uplift'. This is when rocks gradually rise upwards to form mountains. Because we are fixated on her boobs, every time she says 'uplift', various people rock and snort with bottled-up laughter. Mrs Mills can't understand it. She keeps saying, 'What's so funny about uplift?' and when she says, 'Mountains don't just pop up out of nowhere . . .', Dylan Pocky, who is the class psychopath, explodes like the cap being taken off a giant, shaken-up Coke bottle.

When she holds up a picture of two gigantic balls of granite standing next to each other and asks, 'Can anybody make a comment about these?' Dylan falls off his seat and rolls around the floor with his face red and the veins on his forehead sticking out. He gets sent to the Principal.

At lunch, Vince and I eat our sandwiches on the library steps. As usual, I moan to Vince about home, and as usual, he calms me down. Vince is my best friend. Correction. Vince is my only friend.

In English, Mr Bergonzi has got together all these extracts from books about weird families. I suppose this is to make us feel good about our own. He should meet mine.

Then it's Computer Studies—bliss! I ask the teacher for more programming exercises.

After school, Cordelia is putting up a spectacular poster she's made for the dance. As if we need to be reminded. *Tiff's outfit*! My blood runs cold at the thought of it. This dance is going to be a nightmare—unless Vince is there.

'You going to the dance?' Vince asks. I beam at him. Vince is the best.

As I walk down the jetty, Col and Clem run heavily up the beach. They tell me that Blanche and Grandpa had a huge argument and Grandpa stormed off to the mainland to change his will. This happens about five times a year, but Col and Clem always get worried.

Their pale blue eyes blink anxiously behind their specs like startled chicks. Their shovel hands are green and soft from years of handling kelp. They look as if they're permanently wearing gloves. Their big, orange-freckled arms are blurred with curly golden down. When I was a kid I used to pat those furry arms. They used to hold my hand, one on each side, and swing me through the air. There are big Tates, like Col and Clem, and there are skinny Tates, like me. The big ones worry.

Twins run in the family. In the old days they often didn't make it. Col and Clem were born prematurely and their brains got starved of oxygen. While this made them slow, it also burnt out every mean bit in them. Col and Clem don't have a rotten bone in their big lumbering bodies. Which is bad because I do.

I mean, I love Col and Clem. But they drive me mad because they're always entering competitions and getting me to think of slogans and fill in the forms. I quite often avoid them. Then I feel guilty for days.

But they never seem to notice. Or if they do, they don't hold it against me.

I fill in their latest form and think up a slogan for 'Why I want to party on at Club Med New Caledonia'. I have a vision of Col and Clem sitting by a posh resort pool in their black shorts and rubber boots. They're beaming. Their big bums are spilling over the tiny white plastic seats. They're holding those cocktails that have little paper umbrellas. Small children are dumbfounded. Everyone's dumbfounded.

I head for my room. Sanctuary. It's the

one room in the house that's neat and tidy. I've painted all my heavy wooden furniture white. On the dressing-table mirror is a photo of the Wall Street Stock Exchange that I tore out of a magazine at the dentist's. Facing it on the wall is my Year Eight Commerce assignment: 'Great Bankers and Financiers'. It's got heaps of newspaper cuttings stuck on a piece of pale blue cardboard, plus a graph comparing people's various achievements. I used to have all my clippings of Mr Murdoch pinned on the walls, but now I've got them in a scrapbook.

Rupert Murdoch strides into the kelp factory, takes one long penetrating look, and calls for Emily. 'Emily, the trick of success is the ability to delegate. You know the kelp business, what would you suggest?'

'Emily, go and get that silly old coot down to dinner immediately.' It's Blanche at my door, red-faced. I can tell she really needs me to pass the notes.

Grandpa's office is situated in the factory at the top of some stairs. It sticks out over the vats below like the bridge on a ship. Which was probably Great-Great Grandpa's intention. The office is amazingly untidy—as you would expect since nothing has been put away for thirty years. It is a business person's nightmare.

It also has a strange, socky, leafy smell. For years I thought this was Grandpa. But once, when I was asked to try and find some documents, I discovered that all the documents on the bottom layer are actually biodegrading. I think this is because of the heat and steam coming up from the bubbling kelp underneath. When I told Vince, he said it accounted for the leafy smell. But he reckoned the socky smell was definitely Grandpa.

Grandpa is skinny, small and practically bald. He has orange freckles on the top of his head and tufts of white and red hair protruding from his ears. He sits at his desk wearing rubber boots and two pairs of glasses because his eyes are so weak. His bony elbows stick out. He's too mean to buy himself a stronger pair.

A pair of glasses, that is—not elbows, or rubber boots. He's probably also too mean to buy himself a new pair of rubber boots, if it comes to it, but we don't need any more rubber boots on the island. When people die their boots get recycled. I think the pair I'm wearing at the moment belonged to my Great-Auntie Sadie. She died when her bike crashed into an albatross. Or maybe an albatross crashed into her bike. Either way, the bike was a mess.

Grandpa's frowning.

'Excuse me, Grandpa, it's time for dinner.'

He keeps working for a while, then looks up.

'What did she call me?'

'Just an old coot, Grandpa.'

Grandpa smiles and tuts triumphantly. He counts it a victory when Blanche comes up with one as obvious as that. Sometimes I think Grandpa lives for revenge.

As we come out of the factory, Grandpa stops and looks at it with pride. 'One day, Emily, I will be leaving this to you. For later generations.'

I look at the rusty tin roof, the kelp-stained walls, the aunties' broken armchairs scattered over the grass and I think, 'Thanks a lot, Grandpa.'

In our dining room, generations of Tates

stare down at us through their specs. We probably got the Australian spectacles industry going. We must have made dozens of optometrists rich.

I've just removed a heap of laundry from my chair and sat down when Blanche writes the first note. 'You're not getting any ice-cream until you give us more money for housekeeping, you old moron.'

I pass it to Grandpa who writes back, chewing up a storm. 'I'm not giving good money to be spent on gold fillings, you red-nosed drongo.'

'I do not spend money on gold fillings,' Blanche writes back. (This is true. Rod, the dentist on the mainland, is infatuated with her and keeps putting them in for free.) 'If you weren't such a dim old fool . . .'

This goes on for the entire meal, which is a stunningly bad version of fish fingers and instant mash. Don't ask me how you mess up fish fingers and instant mash, because I don't know, but Tiff can do it.

Anyway, everything is going normally. This is like a million other dinners we've all had. As usual, after the meal, I get a bowl of hot kelp for Grandpa's feet—for bunions developed, he claims, by years of poorly fitting rubber boots. As he lowers in his horny feet with a sigh of luxury, he goes into his usual routine about what a cantankerous woman Blanche is. About how I am the only one with a spark of business sense and how Blanche would ruin the business if left to herself. About how Blanche will be sorry when he is dead, because *then* she will get her come-uppance.

He gives his usual chesty cackle.

He coughs.

He turns red, then grey.

His head drops.

'Mum?' I call. Then, more urgently, 'Mum! Quick! I think Grandpa's . . .'

'You think Grandpa's what?' says Blanche, striding up, ready for a re-match. She stops in her tracks.

'Dad?' Her voice is soft and wobbly. It must be the first time in ten years she's spoken to him in the house. She reaches out a hand. As she touches him, his glasses drop off into the bowl of kelp with a hollow and final gloop.

Grandpa is dead. And what's more, as we later discover, he's left the factory to his brother in England, my elderly Great-Uncle John.

Chapter 4

Ms Emily Tate
Tate Island
Victoria
Australia

Dear Ms Tate,

Mr Murdoch thanks you for your kind
letter and wishes you every success in
your chosen career.

Yours sincerely,

F W Paterson

For and on behalf of
Rupert Murdoch

Grandpa is buried in the island graveyard. The Reverend Syd Tate does the ceremony and a hundred Tates stand with spectacles bowed. It looks like a commercial for a multicultural optometrist. I stare around. It's frightening. There's definitely something to this inbreeding thing. Give us a hundred years and we'll all be born with green hands and webbed feet. Actually, Auntie Ruby's feet are already webbed. Make that fifty.

Everyone comes back to the house for refreshments. Tiff brings out a mountain of wet tomato sandwiches. There's a mass exodus to the ferry.

Vince stays. We walk along the beach, skirting the nastier seals. There must be over two hundred seals. Bonzo, Black Ear, Whiskers, Fangs, we know all of them. They like to arrange themselves around the stumps of the Endangered Species noticeboards put up by the Department of Wildlife.

For years the Wildlife people replaced these boards. As soon as the ranger left, the seals would charge at the noticeboards, topple them and gnaw them to bits. The Department gave up when one of their rangers got mauled. Now they tell us it's our responsibility.

Frankly, I reckon anyone coming to hunt our seals can take their chances.

The factory has been shut down out of respect. I've never known the vats not to be churning. The lines of drying seaweed lift and fall in the breeze. In the distance we can see Clem and Col standing outside the factory. They work every day of the week, so they're uncertain how to cope with not doing anything. They're still in their suits. Their hands hang out of the sleeves like big green steaks.

We sit on a rock that has fossils embedded in it and stare out to sea. Vince says that the souls of dead fishermen come back as seagulls. We wonder whether Grandpa counts as a fisherman. Vince tosses a bit of Tiff's tomato sandwich at a flock of gulls. Two of them swoop to get it.

They start that squawking, pop-eyed thing. They run at each other with tipped-back heads and throats all thick with rage. One chokes it down and flies off gagging. The other goes ballistic with rage and runs in a circle. No question. Grandpa's a seagull.

I see Vince off in his boat and go back to the house. Tiffany is scraping plates full of sandwiches into a bucket for the chooks and whingeing. But her heart's not in it. Poor Tiff. I give her a hug. As I turn on the taps to re-wash the china, I think of Mr Murdoch's letter and get depressed. But after all, from his point of view, why should he adopt me? He doesn't know I'm top of my class in commerce. He doesn't know I made two million pretend dollars in that exercise we did on the stock market. How could he? But if he saw my school report...

Mr Rupert Murdoch
News Limited
United States of America

Dear Mr Murdoch,

Further to my request for adoption, I enclose my latest school report plus two merit certificates for outstanding achievement in commerce.

Yours sincerely,

Emily Tate

I post the letter as the sun is setting, and go to find Blanche. She's sitting alone in the office staring at Grandpa's chair. She looks at me, red-eyed. 'I suppose,' she sighs, 'I suppose we should open the will ...'

'That crazy vindictive old sod!'

'Blanche ...'

'That mean-spirited, evil, malicious old ratbag!'

It's 3.00 am, we're in Vince's living room and Blanche is ripping into poor George. Vince and I are hovering in case she attacks him.

'Blanche, I was his solictor!'

'So that permits you to rewrite his will in favour of *Uncle John*! Who hasn't been *heard of* for fifty years! Change back that will!'

'No I will not!'

'Then invent a new one!'

Suddenly the door flies open and standing there is the only Tate on earth more cantankerous than Blanche. She's eighty-five, she's Koori, and she's George's mum, Nanny Ethel.

'What the blazes d'you two think

you're screaming about! Blanche, the old man was entitled to leave the factory to whoever he wanted. Now go home!'

'I will not!'

Nanny Ethel boils.

'Oh, that father of yours spoilt you! Too used to getting your own way, that's your trouble, madam! The one time poor little Tiff gets anything . . .'

Vince and I gasp. Nanny Ethel is mentioning *Tiff's* share!

The point is, Grandpa hasn't exactly left the factory to Uncle John. It's worse. Uncle John gets forty-five per cent, *I* get ten per cent (*me*!), and Tiff—'Tiffany!' screeches Blanche when she hears—Tiff, who hasn't set foot in the factory for thirty years, and who wouldn't know a receipt from a bar of soap, *gets the remaining forty-five*.

But Blanche just sniffs in a martyred way. 'It's all right for you, Ethel. I've just lost my livelihood. That is *my* factory, *my* career, and I will not be fobbed off with a measly ten per cent!'

I nearly choke with outrage. *Her* ten per cent!

I fold my arms and start fuming. This is so typical of Blanche. I don't exist. Well.

We shall see. Perhaps I just won't take it any more. Perhaps I'll side with Uncle John!

You see, what none of them seems to realise is that if it comes to a fight between Uncle John and Tiff . . . *I hold the deciding vote!*

Chapter 5

The late night means I'm sleepy all through school the next day. But as soon as the final bell rings I'm wide awake. This is because I have an urgent dental appointment. I'm not sure that I need an urgent dental appointment. In fact, I'm pretty sure I don't, because I have had five urgent dental appointments in three weeks. The problem is that Rod the dentist is in love with Blanche.

Rod's mega-crush started after Blanche invited him to the Australia Day dance. He doesn't know there was no-one else available. Anyway, as a direct result of Rod's passion, I have had every millimetre of my teeth inspected many times over. In fact, I have been tapped, scraped, picked at, flossed, filed down, brushed and covered in fluoride at least once and some-times more. I have also received three Kermit the Frog toothbrushes, two Miss Piggy toothbrushes and one Bananas-in-Pyjamas toothbrush (B1). And Rod still hasn't plucked up the courage to invite her out. All I can say is, I'm glad he's not a surgeon.

As it is, if this goes on much longer, my teeth will be completely worn away like the rocks in Geology after the Ice Age. Fortunately, last week Rod had a brain-wave. He says I need a plate.

So now, as Blanche raves on about Grandpa, Rod has my mouth propped open with something. It feels like a mini-ature mouth organ. He's supposed to be taking an impression of my teeth for a plate, but he's just standing next to me staring in a dazed way at Blanche. This is even more embarrassing because Rod, I might say, is short, stocky and about fifty. He has a pot belly that strains at his white dentist's smock. He also has a lot of trouble with his hair. Not the hair on his head, the rest.

It's not just that his hands and his arms are hairy, or that there's this big grey doormat fighting to climb over his collar.

His eyebrows—which I've had a lot of opportunity to stare at—are incredible! I used to think they were like those furry caterpillars, but they're actually more bristly than that. They're so bristly you feel you could pick them off his face and use them to brush the fluff off your blazer.

However, the most amazing things are his ears. They have these huge lumps of black and white fluff sticking out of them. On the rare occasions he leans over to do something to my mouth, I stare at them in fascination. How can he not notice them? It looks like a couple of baby hamsters just ducked in there and died.

But he's so devoted to Blanche that you have to feel sorry for him. His mouth hangs open, rapt. He tugs it up and down in response to her comments—a laugh, a sigh. Sometimes he gets it wrong and has to smother a laugh or pull a frown into a manly chuckle. He's not listening at all. He's just watching her like an adoring old labrador.

'To Uncle John . . .!' declaims Blanche.

Rod tuts and shakes his head.

'How is an eighty-five-year-old man supposed to run a factory!'

Rod nods in disgust.

'And what about Tiffany?'

Rod turns his nod to a bitter snort.

'I mean, *Tiffany*!'

Rod tosses his eyes to heaven, drops his head, shakes it, tuts, slaps a hand against his thigh, bites his lip and sighs. I guess he's been looking forward to seeing her.

Blanche tells him how all the solicitors in the town are gutless because they won't change the will. How the Citizens' Advice Bureau are incompetent because they didn't serve her first. I give up when she starts on about Grandpa's doctor. How he's obviously a crook because he refused to sign a document saying that Grandpa was insane. I stare at the bobbly grey concrete on the ceiling.

I'm just at the bit where Emily Enterprises is taking America by storm when Rod shoves a U-shaped plastic trough of pink gunk up onto my teeth. I nearly choke. Not because of the trough but because Rod forgets to remove his hand from my mouth. He's entranced by Blanche. She's vowing that if Uncle John ever tries to set foot on the island she will drive him out. She'll refuse him access to the office! She'll disconnect the phone!

She'll make the family go on strike!

She beams maliciously and swings her short-sighted gaze about the room. The beam accidentally hits Rod. He lights up. Life surges into him. He bends and sways.

'Well,' he chuckles, 'if the worst comes to the worst we'll just have to give him some periodontal flap surgery!'

I'm dribbling, but like Blanche I'm interested.

'Some periodontal what? What's that?'

'What is it!' He's positively jolly. 'It's just about the most horrific bit of dentistry you can go through, that's what it is!'

'Really? Why?'

Rod folds his arms across his white smock. He sets his legs astride. He's showing off. He looks like one of those dentists in TV commercials except I can see up his nostrils.

'Well, we have to cut the gum, peel it back in flaps, then pack the gums and sew them up. You're out of action for six months.'

'Out of action?'

'Yes! Can't eat, shocking pain, it's diabolical!'

He laughs heartily and snaps down the trough. My teeth! Still there.

'Rinse now.'

My mouth feels like it's been dusted with talc. My tongue's waving aimlessly like those stumpy black things you see inside budgies' beaks. I gulp in some green stuff, gargle and spit. As I look up from the swirling basin I notice that Rod's uneasy.

'Of course,' he's saying, swallowing, 'you'd never do it on a healthy mouth.'

'Oh, of course not,' says Blanche.

'I mean, it would be a criminal offence to do it on a healthy mouth,' blusters Rod.

'Except as a last resort.'

Rod and I are equally appalled. Rod stops in his tracks and stares. Then looks away, flustered.

'With a bit of luck the dental technician can start on Emily's plate first thing,' he says brightly. 'Then she can have it by the weekend! Every moment counts now of course. Since it's been left so long.'

He's fussing around guiltily. He flicks the switch on the chair. As I'm cruising upright I see Blanche is smiling.

'You're a wicked man.'

She's flirting. Spare me . . .

'Just my little joke,' says Rod anxiously. He hesitates. He's about to ask her.

Ask her, for heaven's sake! It's not as if she's got anything better to do on a Saturday night. Besides which, you're eroding my molars.

He chickens out.

'So. I think I should see Emily next Thursday.'

'You cannot do that to Uncle John!'

'Do what? Emily, it was a joke!'

We're striding along the corridor out of Rod's surgery. We pass his partner's surgery. Her name is Vicki and she is a bit of a rebel. It's hard to understand why she went into dentistry because it's not really a career where you can do much rebelling. Vicki manages by criticising fluoride. She also hands out green eucalyptus twigs and little packets of salt instead of Sesame Street toothbrushes. She used to be Grandpa's dentist. They fell out when she asked him whether he wanted to save the planet and Grandpa replied, 'Bugger the planet.'

Today, I stop in amazement outside Vicki's surgery. Because, inside, there is a truly frightening sight. It is my distant cousin, Lauren Tate. She is acting as Vicki's assistant. She is staring vacantly into space. In her hand is a little hose that is poked into some poor unsuspecting old lady's mouth. I really like Lauren. The problem is she comes from another planet.

Lauren is two years older than me. Her nickname is 'Lo-Lo'. Vince and I call her 'Oh no, Lo-Lo'. This is because everything Lo touches is a disaster. When you see her, your first words are always, 'Oh no!'

Even for a Tate, she's weird. It's as if there's some powerful force working on her. Something like gravity—except that instead of dragging her towards the earth, it's dragging her towards disaster. Whatever this force is, nothing is easy for Lo. Plates fall, shoes trip up, paint spills. Lo stands on a beach in front of a perfectly calm sea. A monster wave immediately comes out of nowhere and drenches her. Lo goes into a shop to buy some clothes. The rail of the curtain in the changing room falls and concusses her.

With all this in mind, you can imagine that seeing Lo acting as a dental nurse is truly terrifying. I think, 'Oh no!'

Lo notices us. She waves! From the muffled screams of the old lady, I can tell she's altered her grip on her little vacuum hose. She's vacuuming the old lady's cheek. Lo says, 'Oh sorry!'

Another of Lo's nicknames is 'Oh sorry!'

As Lo fixes my next appointment, she tells us how she's going to be doing her two-week work experience as a dental nurse in Rod's surgery. She starts on Saturday. Rod says she could come in for a few hours today, just to get the idea. She says how excited she is about it. She explains how the moment Rod heard her name was Tate, he gave her the job.

Oh Rod, I hope you're well insured . . .

Blanche and I are arguing on our way to the ferry. She infuriates me the way she thinks I know nothing about business.

'Mum, I know heaps about commerce and economics! I've got loads of ideas to improve the business. When Uncle John comes . . .!'

'Emily, Uncle John is not coming, and the business has been doing very well as it is for generations. If by any chance the old fool does turn up, Tiff and I can over-rule him. Thank heavens Dad had the sense to leave me ten per cent!'

'He left *me* ten per cent!'

Oops. Said it. *Damn.*

Blanche stops and looks at me for a moment. Then she snorts and walks on.

I see red.

'He did! They're my shares, not yours!'

'Emily, you're fourteen. He left you those shares to punish me!'

I stare at her. I feel tears. *Mr Murdoch, I need you!*

Blanche goes all guilty and awkward.

'Look, Em, when you're a bit older . . .'

But I run. I run all the way to the ferry. I *can* do it! I *can* run the business! But I'm cut. Because deep down I know she's right. And I hate her for making me know it.

The ferry passes Nanny Ethel and a couple of little old ladies in a battered motor boat. They're on their way to the North Beach. Nanny and her friends are the only people apart from Vince and me who go there. They fish and listen to the races.

We walk in the house. Tiff rushes up, unbearable. Blanche and I prickle in unison.

'Blanche!'

'Not now!' growls Blanche.

'But Blanche ...'

'Not *now*, Tiffany, I ...'

'Blanche, it's Uncle John!'

'What? You don't mean he's ... dead?'

Blanche is glowing.

'No, of course he's not dead!' Tiff's giggling girlishly.

'He's arriving on Friday morning!'

Chapter 6

Please don't let them see me . . .

   'All right, Blanche, foot down!'

   Please don't let them see me . . .

The truck is revving and shaking. Blanche is at the wheel and Martin is standing on the running board.

   Whoever there is out there, deity, Grandpa . . . On second thoughts, not Grandpa . . .

   Our truck is huge and forty years old. It's kept running by Cousin Martin. He's the only one who can drive it because half the gears are missing and you can't get the parts. Except, this morning, Blanche is driving. And I'm dressed like Dorothy in *The Wizard of Oz*.

   'Nurse her, Blanche! Rock the clutch!'

Blanche is trying to get the truck up the ramp onto the barge. In reverse. In reverse because this is the only slow gear that still works. On to the barge so she and I can get to the airport and claim Uncle John before George. I'm crammed into this outfit so Uncle John will warm to my childish innocence. The final touch is my dental plate. Rod screwed me into it with pliers. He promises I'll stop frothing in a day or two.

The truck gives an almighty roar and rolls forward down the ramp.

'Rock the clutch! Reverse! Slowly!'

Martin bellows. He's a skinny Tate.

Blanche frantically rams the gear stick about. She finds reverse. Magic. The truck stops, then, with the engine revving higher and higher, proceeds majestically backwards up the ramp. The side of the truck reads TATE ISLAND KELP in red letters splattered seaweed-brown ...

'Whoa!'

Thump! The truck drops heavily on the barge, bouncing creakily. Blanche is triumphant. Martin's anxious.

'Remember. Never completely stop. If you stop, you stall. If you do stall, you'll have to start her in reverse ...'

'Yes, yes.' Blanche never listens. 'Hop in, Em.'

Blanche is rocking the truck back and forth. I take a leap. I wonder how we'll get Uncle John in.

Ruby sets the barge in motion. We pull away slowly. Martin's standing on the wharf yelling instructions. Blanche isn't listening. I sink down in my seat. At least it's a day off school.

Please don't let anyone from school be there.

The wharf's empty. I brighten. I jump out and give Blanche instructions to unload. The sun's coming up and the truck is chugging healthily. The Year Eleven football team comes jogging round the corner.

Let me die.

Mr Rupert Murdoch
News Limited
United States of America

Dear Mr Murdoch,

I am writing in the hope that you will give me some advice on my current

*position. I have recently inherited ten per
cent of my family business and wish to
revitalise it. I have two partners. One is
thirty-five and knows nothing about the
business. One is eighty-five, knows
nothing about the business and is
possibly senile. I am fourteen.*

Yours sincerely

Emily Tate

The sun's high and we're steaming along
the main highway. Literally. Forty years'
worth of baked kelp gives off an incredible
smell. People in overtaking cars crane their
necks, horrified. I suck my plate. Blanche
clutches the wheel, frowning. Not that
she's angry. Just that she can't see.

'What does that say? Milton? Where
the hell's Milton?'

'Melbourne.'

'To the left?'

'No, straight! Straight ahead! Mind
that car!'

We go around the roundabout twice.
People lean on their horns.

'What cheek! It's my right of way!'

Blanche fumes. She yells out in a cracked voice, 'It's my right of way, you ignorant roadhog!'

Her long, dangly earrings swing madly. Her fluffy red hair sticks out like a dandelion clock. I think longingly of Jennifer Blake's mother. Soft voice. Secretary of the P&C. Designer tracksuits.

'Remember to kiss him.'

'What?'

'Uncle John. Remember to kiss him.'

'Oh, what . . .!'

'Go up. Kiss him. I don't care whether you never kiss him in your life again, but kiss him this morning. I need him softened up . . .'

'Mum, I . . .'

I stop. Terror.

'Mum, traffic lights!'

We can't stop because the truck will stall.

They're green. Blanche accelerates. They turn amber. Blanche swears and rams her foot to the floor. The lights turn red. We scream in unison and go hurtling through.

For thirty seconds we drive in silence.

'Anyhow. Kiss him.'

At the airport it occurs to us that I will have to meet Uncle John alone because we can't park the truck.

'Remember to hold up the sign.'

'Yes, Mum.'

'And remember to carry his luggage.'

'Yes, Mum.'

The truck-engine is screaming because we're going at a snail's pace in third gear in front of the terminal.

'And for heaven's sake, stop doing that sucking, clicking thing with your plate.'

I open the door and jump.

'I'll keep circling the carpark. I'll honk!'

Like, I'm going to miss her . . .

Emily was bored with international air travel. Another trip to New York . . . ! Eddie was wheeling her custom-made luggage respectfully behind her. To him, the future loomed bleak. Three weeks without Emily. It would be hard to bear. Even harder than the knowledge that Brett Harper had proposed and Emily was considering the offer. What had he, a humble carpark attendant, to offer the magnificent Emily . . .

Oh what's the use. I'm fourteen, skinny. I've got a mouth full of wire and I'll never go on an international flight in my life.

If I stick my tongue under the curved bit of the plate I can flick the whole thing up and down. It hurts like hell but I can't stop doing it.

His plane landed twenty minutes ago. The automatic doors from the customs area slide open and close. People come out grinning behind loaded trolleys. Squeals of excitement and reunions. I hold up the cardboard sign reading 'Mr John Tate'.

An old lady gets pushed out in a wheelchair. I suppose Uncle John will come out in a wheelchair. An entire rugby team comes out in matching jackets.

Here he is. In a wheelchair. An air hostess by his side. Being pushed by a gorgeous young guy in white slacks and sunglasses who's chatting up the air hostess. Uncle John's head is drooped and lolling. He's chewing toothless gums. He has a few strands of greasy grey hair plastered over his bald head.

I have to kiss him. I cannot kiss him. I cannot go anywhere near him.

I hold the cardboard sign over my face and panic.

'Excuse me. Are you waiting for John Tate?'

It's the gorgeous young guy. Black hair. Perfect teeth.

I nod. I cover my mouth so he won't see the plate.

'Oh jolly good!'

He smiles and takes off his sunglasses. Green eyes. Dark eyelashes.

I worship him. I want to beg him to help me. To give me money to run away. I want to explain that if I have to kiss Uncle John I will scream hysterically and puke.

He puts out his hand.

'I'm John Tate. I'm *so* pleased to meet you.'

I'm aware of sharp pain and a draft on my teeth. This is because my jaw is hanging open and my plate is half-flicked. I stare at the young man. I flick back my plate. I notice that the old man in the wheelchair has been claimed by a group of nuns.

John is looking at me closely, still smiling.

'Are you all right?' he asks.

It suddenly occurs to me. I have to kiss

him. I let out a great snort of a laugh that sounds like a belch.

Now John's really concerned.

'Excuse me . . .'

Get a grip. (I'd like to get a grip on you! Ha! Ha!) What is the matter with me? I'm going crazy! Uncle John is young and gorgeous!

'No, you see . . . I wasn't expecting you to be . . . I thought . . . I thought . . . you'd be old. I thought you were that man in the wheelchair . . .'

'Oh! I see!'

John chuckles. (To die for. Chuckle again!) I start to chuckle. He chuckles. We shake hands. Soon I'm doubled-up with hysterical laughter and he's looking a bit startled again. I take a punt and explain.

'I thought I had to kiss that old man.'

'Oh right! Oh *dear*! No, no, the air hostess just needed a hand.' Now we're chuckling conspiratorially. 'Look, I'm sorry, are you a relative?'

'I'm Emily. Grandpa was . . . well he was my grandpa.'

'John Tate was my grandfather. My father's dead, so the inheritance came to me.'

'You don't look like a Tate.'

Major understatement. He looks like a god. There's a purring little ringing sound from his pocket. He gets out ... *a mobile phone*! I hear the 'Hallelujah Chorus'. He beams.

'Do excuse me. Hello? Oh Hi, David! Yes, I've just landed. *Bloody* hot! Mm. Oh hell, no! Sell them! The market's going to go down much further than this!'

He smiles at me and covers the phone.

'Sorry. My stockbroker.'

He grimaces charmingly and walks away, talking. I'm in a dream. He's young and gorgeous. And a businessman.

Chapter 7

When we get out to the carpark we see
Blanche. She is leaning out of the truck's
cabin arguing with George, who's on foot.
The truck is at the head of a traffic jam.
Cars are honking. Not because the argument is very heated, but because it's being
conducted with the truck going slowly in
reverse.

George sights us and comes up anxiously. He's bewildered at the sight of
John. He looks at me for an explanation.

'Uncle John's dead, Uncle George. This
is John Tate, his grandson.'

'Oh!' George beams and sticks out his
hand.

'I'm George Tate, your cousin, old Mr
Tate's solicitor.'

'Emily!'

It's Blanche, bellowing as the truck crawls backwards around the corner at the head of its convoy of honking vehicles.

'Excuse me.'

I hurry over to her.

'Go back in and get Uncle John!'

'That is Uncle John. I mean, it's John Tate, Uncle John's grandson.'

'Where's Uncle John, then?'

'He's dead. Cousin John inherited his share.'

'Oh did he,' says Blanche cynically. 'We'll soon see about that!'

A taxi has its front bumper pushed up to the truck's. The driver leans out of his window.

'Tell that old chook with the earrings to get her truck out of the way!'

'I heard that, you big ape!'

Blanche has to trade insults at the same time as looking in her rear-vision mirror. It occurs to me that she is trapped.

'I have to go.'

'Emily, come back!'

I dash off, pretending not to hear. George can give us a lift back. He's leaning over to pick up John's suitcase. John's staring at the traffic jam. He's trying to suppress a smile.

'George, that person in the reversing truck ...'

Blanche is yelling. The taxi driver leans on his horn. Blanche leans on her horn. The entire traffic jam leans on its horns.

George and I cringe. George coughs.

'That's your second cousin Blanche.'

'Oh so *that's* Blanche. She's a total loony isn't she?'

'She's er ... well, she's Emily's mother.'

John's appalled with himself.

'Oh dear. I do apologise.'

I shrug, glad it's out in the open. 'She's not mad exactly. She just goes berserk when she doesn't get her own way. She wants to give you a lift back to the island.'

'No, *I'm* taking him,' exclaims George.

But John smiles.

'Actually, it's not a problem. I've got a hire car.'

He holds up the keys. George is flustered.

'Oh no, John, we couldn't let you drive! You don't even know the way.'

'Then Emily can show me. If she'd be so kind.'

Would I ever! John's picking up his

things. George is blustering but John is charming.

'Really, old chap, it's no trouble. I always drive myself. Come along, Em.'

Em!

I grab a bag and follow. George is left speechless. The last thing I see of Blanche is her waving, frantic hand as the truck reverses behind some trees.

The hire car is a Porsche. Exactly like Emily's but red.

After the truck, its engine's so quiet I feel as if I've gone deaf. The road rolls up and away in the reflections on John's sunglasses. His shirt sleeves are rolled. I'm amazed at the normality of his forearms. Tate men usually have arms like hairy sticks or Christmas hams.

'It's funny, this,' he says.

'Being in Australia?'

'No, driving on this side of the road. I've been in France for six months.'

He overtakes a Merc, tossing back a lock of his black hair. He's from another world. How can somebody like this even consider Tate Island? Perhaps he's not. Perhaps he is going to sell us out.

'John.'

'Mm?'

'Why are you coming to Tate Island?'

He grins.

'Dunno, really. Seemed like a good idea at the time.'

He smiles at me. I can't see his eyes. He's impossibly good-looking.

'Why, Em? Don't you want me here?'

I turn to the speeding paddocks.

'Blanche says you'll sell us out.'

'Why should I do that?'

He's genuinely surprised.

I burst out, 'But what is there for someone like you on Tate Island?'

'Well.' He's amused. 'Maybe I can make the factory more profitable. I do have some experience, you know.'

'What experience?'

He throws back his head and laughs.

'Good girl! Good business head! Never take assertions like that on trust!'

He's pulled off the road. We're parked outside an incredibly posh restaurant. He turns to me.

'It's lunchtime. I'll make a deal. I'll tell you absolutely everything you want to know about my qualifications and experience, if you answer me one question.'

I look at him.

'Why the hell are you dressed like Dorothy in *The Wizard of Oz*?'

Chapter 8

The restaurant has white tablecloths, a low hum of voices, and a whole cutlery tray of knives and forks in front of each place.

We are given menus the height of a brick wall. I remember I'm supposed to remove my plate for eating. How should I do it? When? Worse, what should I do with it once it's out?

I consider casually placing it on one of the side plates. I decide to keep it in.

John orders for both of us in French. He gets wine and asks me if I'd like a glass with my meal. I shrug elegantly, as if this is perfectly normal. It tastes horrible. It's sort of nutty sour and stings my sore gums. But the food is exquisite. It's so unlike any food Tiff's ever cooked I can't even identify what animal it comes from.

I get some salad that's about ninety per cent bean sprouts and cress and ten per cent some leaves I've never seen before. It tastes of nothing but you can tell it's really sophisticated.

I explain about the dress. John hoots with laughter. I ask questions and try to use the right cutlery. He tells me how he was born in Paris but went to boarding school in England. He got bored with school, so he left and went into his step-father's electronics business in France. He says they also have a vineyard. He started his own company in London at twenty-two. He sold it eighteen months later for a huge profit. He's now twenty-eight. He talks about share portfolios and bonds.

It's all so much like my Emily day-dreams that I have to fight hard to keep my mouth from dropping open. This is especially important because it feels as if there are bean sprouts and cress dangling from the front wire of my plate. There are definitely some trapped under the plastic bit that fits into the roof of my mouth.

When John bends over to get the wine out of the ice bucket I snatch up a silver spoon and bare my teeth. I freeze. There's a whole hanging vegetable garden in there!

I look as if I've just been grazing! Just as John raises his head, I rip out the plate and put it in my lap.

You are not supposed to rip out your plate. This is partly because it might damage your teeth. It is also because most of the skin on your gums comes off with it. I'm in agony. My mouth is one giant, pulsing throb.

John beams and says, 'More wine?'

I smile with my lips closed, in case my mouth is filling up with blood. John pours some more wine in my glass.

'Well, then, let's drink a toast. To Tate Island!'

Oh no! If I don't drink a toast it looks as if I don't want him on the island. If I do, I will burn my gums back to the bone. John raises his glass. He melts me with his gorgeous smile. I mumble, 'Tate Island!' I gulp down some wine. Nothing happens. Then my gums blaze. It feels as if the skin is peeling back as far as my brain. I clench my teeth to stop my lips writhing. My right eye half closes.

At least alcohol is a good disinfectant.

But the pain subsides after a while. Especially since there is John to distract me. A woman goes past with her left arm clamped against her side like a chicken wing. Her hand dangles limply in front. It looks really elegant. I try putting my elbow on the table and dangling my wrist. It looks as if I'm trying to do a shadow puppet imitation of a swan. I put it away.

I don't know whether it's the wine or having been up so early or just John, but I'm in a lovely warm daydream. I've suddenly walked into Emily's life. I almost expect Eddie and Conchita to arrive with my handmade pigskin briefcase.

Mr Rupert Murdoch
News Limited
United States of America

Dear Mr Murdoch,

With reference to my request for adoption by you, I'm pleased to inform you that I no longer need to leave Tate Island because John Tate, the famous businessman, is actually my cousin . . .

Yours sincerely,

Emily Tate

'You're miles away.'

I smile stupidly.

'I was thinking about Rupert Murdoch.'

'I met him once. Interesting chap.'

He's met Rupert Murdoch!

'You've *met* Rupert Murdoch ... !'

John smiles.

'Oh, for something like two seconds. He wouldn't know me from Adam.'

I am having lunch with a man who has met Rupert Murdoch. While the rest of the class is slaving over algebra and history, I am sitting in a posh restaurant with an international businessman who looks like a film star and calls me 'Em'.

When it's time to go, I sail through the restaurant doing chicken-wing arm. The head waiter opens the door for me as if I am a queen.

There is now only one thing that I need to know.

'John, do you ever wear glasses?'

He smiles. He opens the car door for me.

'Contacts.'

Please let somebody see me!

The Porsche is drawing up to the wharf. The entire town is deserted. The most amazing arrival I'm ever likely to make in this town and a mystery plague has wiped out the entire population.

Yes! Suddenly, like the answer to my prayers, three school buses draw up and park.

I introduce John to Vince as the whole of Year Nine gawps in the background. The ferry's approaching.

'What about the car?' I ask.

'Oh leave it. The rental people will come and pick it up. P'raps Vince will drop in the keys for me.'

John grins at Vince and chucks him the keys.

The Year Nine Cool set can't believe it. Their dreadlocks bristle with jealousy.

I smile. I wave.

Thank you, deity. Thank you, Grandpa, O Lord of the angry gulls.

Chapter 9

Tate Island is shaped a bit like a pear with one straight side facing out to sea. For some unknown reason the wharf, the processing plant and our house are built on the horrible, swampy end of the island, while the best beach (North Beach) is left totally untouched at the other end. Since Great-Great-Grandpa Tate spent his life trying to wipe out the local wildlife, it can't have been through any love of the environment.

My theory is that it was a typical Tate reaction to making a mistake. Great-Great-Grandpa started to build in the wrong place (probably having mislaid his glasses). Being a Tate, he couldn't bring himself to admit that he was wrong. Whatever caused it, the result is that while one side of the island looks like a shanty town, the other is completely deserted and has the most fantastic, untouched beach in the world. For some weird reason the seals and albatrosses avoid it and it has very little kelp. There are dolphins and wonderful surf. There are seashells and fine white sand.

John and I are on the ferry. Auntie Ruby likes John. She shows it by flicking the controls at lightning speed and aiming the ferry at three men in a fishing boat. They row frantically. We bear down on them, horn blasting. Ruby swings away at the last moment and they get hit by our bow wave. Their violent swearing wafts on the breeze. Ruby chortles and digs John in the ribs.

As we approach the island wharf there's a strange sight. Col and Clem are thudding up and down the jetty waving their arms. Suddenly, Tates start pouring out from everywhere. It's like one of those old cowboy movies where five thousand Apaches ride over the ridge and sit menacingly on their ponies. They're flooding down to the jetty. The sinking sun flares randomly on their glasses. They're all in rubber boots.

I feel a spasm of panic. What is this? Are they going to lynch him? I notice Tiff surrounded by a group of aunties. Tiff's in her best sarong. Without Blanche to protect her she's terrified. Are they all terrified?

As we pull into the jetty, there's a stirring and a muttering. As the ferry ties up, the muttering grows. When John comes out there's a gasp and then there's complete silence. It's really like a Western.

'Uncle John's dead,' I shout.

My voice echoes round the mangroves.

'This is John Tate, his grandson.'

There is stunned silence. The flies buzz. The family is all as amazed as I was. John steps forward like the cowboy hero addressing the assembled tribes.

'Cousins. Because you *are* all my cousins . . . '

I come in peace to all red men.

'My grandfather, John Tate, loved this place. He always wanted to come back.'

He stares around at them all. Then, humbly . . .

'I am also John Tate.' He pauses. 'Thank you for bringing me home.'

A wall of spectacles stares blankly at him.

A young sulky brave just *has* to leap out and shout, 'White man speak with forked tongue', but nobody does. The Tates are a bit short on young sulky braves. They tend to leave for the city when they turn sixteen.

Then someone starts to applaud. It's Clem. Those big green paws can certainly raise a clap. People stir and look around. Col starts to clap. Then Martin, Auntie Dot, Auntie Violet. Everyone's applauding. Ruby hoots the ferry. Tiff, caught up in the drama of the situation, runs forward and hugs him. (Wish I'd done that.) Everyone's rushing forward to hug him, to shake his hand. You almost expect a band to strike up.

Tiff leads John off in triumph at the head of a happy procession of Tates. She gives him a soft gingernut biscuit and a cup of cold, orange tea so strong it makes his eyes crinkle. But John keeps smiling. He's introduced to everyone. He remembers all their names. Not even *family* remembers everyone's names.

It's hours before I can get him away. But it gives me a chance to change out of my *Wizard of Oz* outfit. I try for sophistication. I give up. I cram my fluffy red hair into a ponytail and get into my least ancient jeans.

I take him for a tour of the island in Grandpa's boat. We stroll along the North Beach. I do the chicken-wing walk and try swinging my hips casually like the Cool set. John asks me to tell him about the island.

I tell him how we have sixty-two different sorts of seaweed, three unique species of mosquito, and probably the southernmost mangrove swamps in the world. I explain that the seaweed we process is bull kelp. I describe how the uncles chop huge armfuls from the ocean and take it in boats back to the factory to be dried, cleaned and pulped up with fresh water. And then, because he's so interested, I get carried away. I rave on about the inefficiencies and Mrs Adeline Bogle. I tell how we could save a fortune in transport costs if we sold the kelp dried. I talk about kilns to dry kelp and using tractors instead of uncles. I'm launching into the financial details, when John smiles and holds up his hand for me to stop. My heart sinks. Have I bored him? But he's reaching into his jacket! He gets out an electronic organiser! 'Sorry,' he smiles, 'I have to make a record of all this. Now, Emily, you were saying?'

The smile on my face is threatening to tear it in half.

As the sun sets, John and I sit on the beach. I am talking and he is taking extensive notes.

It is a dream come true.

At last, someone is listening!

The clutch went on Blanche about twenty kilometres along the tollway. She tried waving people down for two hours until a police car was kind enough to stop. The policemen got out of their car with handkerchiefs over their faces.

The truck was left at Geelong. Rod drove his elderly green Citroen down to pick Blanche up. In the absence of anyone to blame about the truck, Blanche blamed Rod about her gold fillings. He spent four hours apologising. They got back to Yarradindi at 3.00 am. Rod rowed her across to the island in the hope of being asked to stay over, but wasn't. Tiff gave him a cup of cocoa without sugar. He made it back to his surgery by 6.00 am.

John has been given Grandpa's old

room. It looks dark and bare without its rows of rubber boots and kelp hooks.

I stretch out in my sleeping bag outside John's door after shifting a tricycle and a heap of Blanche's astrology magazines. I tell myself it's to protect John from Blanche, but I'm kind of hoping that if Blanche turns up he'll be able to protect me.

I drift into an uneasy sleep. I wake up to see Tiff's foot about ten centimetres away from my nose. She's tapping anxiously on John's door.

'John?' she's saying. 'John, wake up!'

I worm up out of my sleeping bag. It's light.

'What's happening, Tiff?' I mutter.

Then I hear a terrible bellow.

Mad-eyed and smelling horribly of kelp, Blanche comes powering up the corridor yelling, 'All right, you miserable imposter, I'll give you five seconds to get out of there, I . . .'

She has seen me. She narrows her eyes. I try to blend into the floorboards.

'Traitor!' she hisses to me.

'Mum, you don't understand . . . !'

Suddenly the door opens. It's John. He's absolutely immaculate in white trousers, white shirt and white hat. He looks like something out of those ice-cream commercials where the girl's lounging about in a fantastic evening dress and some guy wafts up in slow motion and gives her a chocolate ice-cream.

He grins and puts out his hand.

'Hello, Blanche. I'm so pleased to meet you. I'm John Tate, I . . .'

But Blanche snarls back at him.

'You are not John Tate! I've just been making a few phone calls. There is no record of any John Tate except for old John Tate and his son, who are both dead. So, perhaps you'd like to explain to us exactly who you are!'

Blanche folds her arms triumphantly. I look at John. His warm smile has gone tight and cold.

'You're quite right,' he replies. 'My name is not John Tate.'

I gasp.

'It's Jean-Paul Tate-Coteau. My French mother refused to christen me plain "John", and since my father died, I've used my stepfather's surname. Now, if you'll excuse me . . .'

And he walks off.

'Hey! Don't you walk out on me,' Blanche blusters.

She squints ferociously down the hall. Behind her, on the wall, Great-Grand-father Alfred Tate squints ferociously down the hall. Legend has it that he was killed by a hot water tap. I'd always assumed he was scalded, but Tiff reckons he was having an affair with a plumber's wife. The plumber came home early and chucked a tap at him.

But John keeps walking. Blanche is ropeable. She gives a strangled roar and runs out of the back door. She races along the sand, into the factory and up into the office. I chase after her. I come into the office just in time to see her chopping the phone cord in half with scissors. John appears at the door. Blanche cackles and holds the phone and its dangling cord up like a trophy. John blinks and says, 'How terribly inconvenient for you!' And gets out his mobile.

Chapter 10

I catch Auntie Ruby's ferry just in time. I'm dying to tell Vince about everything. I run up into the bus.

'Hey you!'

It's Justin. (Countdown to kelp joke.) But Justin doesn't do a kelp joke at all. He just mumbles, 'Good car . . .'

I'm stunned. This is approval. Justin approves of *me*?

It's all so funny I can't wait to tell Vince. I stride up the aisle doing chicken-wing. I plonk down next to him. He turns to me. He's furious.

'Don't you *ever* do that to me again!'

'Do what? What do you mean?'

'He treated me like a servant!' Vince's mouth is stretched into a hard, thin line. He mimics John's accent.

' "Hee-ah Vince!" Chucks the keys at me!'

'He didn't mean to insult you.'

'Well, he *did*. And you went along with it.'

I suppose I did. We travel in silence. Justin and the Cools are having a burping competition.

The bus stops at the lights. The old man with the bald head and the shorts up to his chest is telling off a policeman.

I turn to Vince.

'Look, Vince . . . maybe they do things differently in England. Or France.'

The bus is pulling up outside our school. Vince is already on his feet.

'Yeah, well.' He snarls. 'He's in Australia now.'

Vince's mouth stays like that all day. I pass him notes about Blanche. I make faces. I offer him a mint. Finally we have a blazing row.

'How can you fall for that smarmy pommy garbage!'

'Get lost!'

'I reckon Blanche is right. I reckon he *is* some kind of imposter!'

'Oh yeah, and you'd know, wouldn't

you! You're just jealous! And don't think I'm coming to the dance with you!'

He stops in his tracks, turns and looks at me. It's the same look he gives me when we're playing Monopoly and I've landed on Park Lane when he's just added two hotels. My heart sinks. I've handed it to him on a plate.

'You *wish*, Emily!'

I feel tears and open my mouth to take it all back. Then I notice something. Vince has folded his arms. He's waiting for me to apologise! I seethe, I start to boil and suddenly I hear someone say 'Loser'. It's Justin, shuffling past on his way to smoke behind the dunnies. He tips his head back and looks out at me from slit eyes.

Of course, I assume he's talking about me. Then I twig. He's talking about Vince. And what's more, he's trying to be friendly!

I have no idea why this is, but what a godsend!

Vince is staring smugly. He's asking for it.

I curl one corner of my lips. I toss back my hair, and in my best gravelly voice, I snarl, 'Nur, Vince, ya try-hard!'

Vince gasps. Justin sniggers.

I think I have become a Cool . . .

Chapter 11

I spend the rest of school re-running the argument in my head. I'm still doing it on the ferry. I'm so taken up with it that when I get to the island, I don't notice what's happening until it's staring me in the face. What is happening is that Blanche is conducting a mass meeting. And she is holding an axe.

Actually, it's a kelp paddle, which means it's time for my next pair of glasses. To explain, a kelp stirring paddle looks a bit like a giant soup spoon. You use it to skim the rubbish off the top of the bubbling kelp. Since this usually consists of plastic bags and bits of fishing line tangled up with dead jellyfish, it is not a popular job. Which is why, until this day, Blanche has never, as far as I know, picked up a kelp paddle in her life. So why today?

My first thought is that she has mistaken it for something else because she's so short-sighted. But as I get closer, I realise that she is waving the paddle about to convince her audience that she is a true, kelp-gathering Tate interested in their welfare. This is because she wants them to go on strike.

The audience is bewildered. This is all so unlike Blanche. Blanche is the person who stands up in the office bellowing insults down at them. They're worried she's lost her marbles.

'To give over our beautiful island to this ignorant foreigner ...' bawls Blanche.

'I think we should call a doctor,' says Auntie Vi.

'To even *consider* letting him stay and take our livelihood ...'

'You're right, Vi, she looks real peaky.' (This is Auntie Dot.)

'I say to you, go on strike! Refuse to work! Refuse to let this stranger, this idle, good-for-nothing Johnny-come-lately ...'

There's a stirring and a murmuring at the back of the crowd that even Blanche can't ignore.

Something is happening. I make my

way through so I can see. One of the little kelp boats is coming in from the ocean. As it reaches shallow water, a man in a white hat and white trousers rolled to the knees jumps out to drag it in. It's John! He's been collecting kelp. He waves cheerfully. In the boat, now in her second-best sarong, is Tiffany.

The crowd bursts out into a round of applause. I do too, but it occurs to me that this clapping is becoming a bit of a thing. Every time John moves he gets a big hand. The trouble is, his behaviour leaves us speechless.

No senior Tate has ever been nice to the family. The senior Tate tactic is yelling and exasperation. And to be honest, when you're dealing with some of the family, yelling and exasperation is the only way to keep sane.

Like when Col loses his glasses in the kelp for about the fifth time in a week and the entire operation has to be shut down while he scoops around apologetically in the vats with a fishing net. Or when Auntie Ruby's favourite chook, Feathers, sits in the middle of the stairs and refuses to move for five days. And Ruby refuses to move her either. Until, that is, Blanche threatens to turn Feathers into a chicken casserole. (Personally, I reckon Feathers' chances are pretty good, because Blanche's idea of cooking is to nag Tiff to make something. But Ruby's not taking risks.)

The point is, we're just not used to people like John being nice. So we clap. Clapping is the only way we have left of expressing approval. Clem whistles through his front teeth. Col copies him. I try, but my tongue's not used to the wedge of plastic on the roof of my mouth. I make a little spurting noise.

The crowd surges down to meet John and adore him. He pulls the boat ashore, swarmed by well-wishers. Cousin Nelly holds up her baby to be blessed.

I suddenly remember Blanche. I turn and look. She's standing there open-mouthed. The kelp paddle is dangling by her side. She narrows her eyes and folds her arms so that the paddle is poking out sideways like a lance. Her face is thunderous. As she strides forward, people leap aside not so much in reverence, but so as to avoid the paddle. It means she cuts an impressive swathe through the crowd.

She gets about three metres away from

John and declaims theatrically, 'Excuse me . . . '

'Oh hello, Blanche. I thought I'd have a look at how you harvest the kelp. It's amazing stuff, isn't it. Spreads for miles!'

He beams. This is not the right response. The right response is to cower and protect your vulnerable bits. All the other Tates immediately have the right response, myself included. Tiffany, sitting in the boat without a hope of concealing herself, looks out to sea in a desperate kind of way, pretending not to exist. But John's breezy.

He dusts the sand off his hands. He puts them on his hips.

'Hard work, that. No wonder you're all so fit and well! What I need now is a good, hot bath!'

Blanche raises an eyebrow. She's staring at him witheringly but just missing. By rights, the ocean just over his left shoulder should turn to stone.

'I would thank you, Mr Whatever-Your-Name-Is, not to engage in business activities without first consulting me.'

John doesn't say anything for a moment, but something tightens in his cheek. He starts to unload the slippery kelp. The silence is electric.

'Why exactly is that, Blanche? As *I* understand it, Tiffany and I are now the directors of the company. Not forgetting Emily, of course. You, I believe, have no position at all.'

You have to give Blanche credit. She doesn't bat an eyelid.

She replies, 'The point is that I'm the only person who knows how to run the office.'

Bad move!

John smiles. 'Quite so. But what I was thinking . . .' he starts dragging the kelp up the beach.

'. . . I was thinking I'd run the place myself.'

He beams. I look at Blanche. A word jumps into my mind.

Gobsmacked.

Chapter 12

John strides off towards the factory. I follow. So does all the family apart from Blanche, who's left staring in astonishment. It feels like Moses leading the children of Israel.

Clem catches up with me. He's excited and dying to tell me something.

'He's been at it all morning, Emily! First he went into the plant. *On the ground level.* Borrowed a pair of boots. He looked in all the vats. Checked all the pipes. Asked us questions. Em, he was *that polite* ... !'

Col has joined him. He's nodding.

'Then he was out in a boat. Of course by now, Tiffany's down to watch and *she* wants to go in the boat. Don't think she's been in a boat for years, Em!'

Ahead of us, John pauses and raises his hand. We all stop.

'Everybody! Please forgive me. I need to start work immediately. I'm very conscious of the fact that I haven't really talked to many of you, so I would like to invite you all, next Sunday, to a party here on the South Beach.'

The applause is deafening. A party! The Tates never have parties. The family breaks up into excited groups and John motions Col, Clem and me to take him into the plant.

We squish through the factory—past the cleaning tanks; past the pulping baths, where the kelp gets turned into greeny-brown sludge and pumped into fat, steaming pipes that pass over our heads and drip green water on us as they carry the kelp to huge vats where its jelly-making ingredient gets isolated. The kelp plops out of a spout into the vats in an unbelievably gross fashion.

It smells like a million fish died after eating brussel sprouts.

I used to bet kids from the mainland five cents they couldn't watch it for ten minutes without feeling sick. Justin was one of the few to survive, but even he looked a bit grey.

But John's not sick. He's not even looking at the vats. He's heading straight for a mass of unsorted seaweed dripping on a line.

'This stuff. I saw it this morning. What can you tell me about it? Is this all the same sort of plant?'

Col steps forward with a smile as wide as a Hallowe'en pumpkin.

'Dead Ear, Corpse's Ribbon, Bobbly Brains, Stink-ball.'

He steps backwards. And salutes. This is a first, but it makes a change from clapping.

John frowns.

'Oh well, that puts paid to that one! I thought we might be able to market them separately under romantic-sounding names. Somehow, Corpse's Ribbon doesn't have quite the right ring.'

I pipe up. 'There are the Aboriginal names.'

'Oh yes? What are they?'

'I don't know, but I know who would. Nanny Ethel.'

'So the Aborigines eat seaweed?'

'Oh no way! They use it for medicines.'

'What kind of medicines?'

'I think they used to suck Bobbly

Brains for sore throats, but it was so disgusting they switched to Strepsils.'

John nods thoughtfully.

'So we have the possibility of gourmet food products, health pharmaceuticals . . .'

'And it's a great face pack and moisturiser,' I burst in, 'if we could only stop it from turning your skin green.'

John closes his personal organiser with a snap.

'Clem, get me a sample of each weed. Col, put each sample in a plastic bag and label it. We'll send them away for analysis. But, unless I'm very much mistaken,' he grins at me, 'we are sitting on a gold mine!'

I grin. I want to dance about. *I have always said this*! Now a real-live business man agrees!

Tiff has cooked a special dinner. Luckily, Blanche is sulking in her room. So John, Tiff, the kids and I sit round the table chewing huge slabs of rubbery steak nestled in lumpy mash and sprinkled with wizened, frozen peas. The steaks have got bands of yellow fat as thick as the inner tubes on a bike. It's certainly a challenge. It's like trying to eat your pillow.

But John tucks in. He says the sea air has given him an appetite. He chats to

Tiffany and is charming to the twins. This is hard because their faces are smeared with gravy and mash. They stare at John with pale blue eyes, breathing heavily. Jeremy's wet little mouth is open in astonishment. Stevie has a pea stuck to the corner of his eyebrow.

After the meal, John and I go up to the office, where somehow John has managed to clear some space. At about 11.00 pm we look up. Blanche is at the door. She says stiffly, 'I came to see if you needed my assistance.'

John replies, very politely, 'No, thank you, Blanche. I think we can manage.'

As he returns to his papers he casually says, 'Oh and Blanche, when I came in earlier I found some of my papers disturbed. You should know that if you sabotage me, you are of course sabotaging the whole family.'

Blanche is rattled. She blusters, 'I did no such thing. I was gathering my belongings, I . . .'

Poor Blanche. She's completely outclassed. I feel a real stab of love and pity for her. Why can't she work *with* John? Why must she always *win*?

She stalks off. John and I settle down

for more conversation. We start to sort out the jumble of papers.

If it wasn't for the smell, I'd be in heaven.

(Just for the record, Vince was wrong. Whatever's responsible for the socky smell, it's certainly not Grandpa. Because it's still here. Mind you, perhaps Grandpa is still here.)

That night I dash off a quick note to Mr Murdoch.

Mr Rupert Murdoch
News Limited
United States of America

Dear Mr Murdoch,

I am just writing to tell you that my partners and I are just about to start renovating our kelp processing plant. Should you wish at any time to visit, please telephone first. If persons called Tiff or Blanche answer, hang up.

Yours faithfully,

Emily Tate

Chapter 13

The next morning John says he's coming to the mainland on the same ferry as me. He needs to do a few things, including posting off the kelp samples. Once they're analysed we'll have a better idea of our potential markets. He tells me he's got his office in London tracking down Japanese experts on kelp. He's very annoyed at Yarradindi beers because they aren't answering his calls. He reckons it's really risky selling everything to the brewery in case they go broke. I suggest I talk to my Japanese teacher about learning to write business letters. John's impressed. I do chicken-wing and say scathing things about the school dance.

At the wharf I'm beaming because once again, the whole of Year Nine sees me with John. I wave him off grandly. As I chicken-wing on to the school bus, Vince is icy. I sit behind Justin. It's the dance tonight. I wonder to myself if I should go on my own. I daydream about hanging around with the Cools, and Vince being furious. Fat chance! Justin might have been strangely friendly yesterday, but the Cools would die rather than have a dag like me in their group. I mean, I'm a dag even in school uniform. In one of Tiff's outfits I'd bring them out in a rash. But the weird thing is that Justin turns around, stares at me and grunts.

I decide to make peace with Vince. I ask him to the dance but he ignores me. I apologise for John and he accepts, but then goes into such an attack on John that we start fighting again and end up having a shouting match next to the Science wing bubblers. He tells me that since John arrived I've got full of myself. He says I'm acting like a Cool.

Just then the Japanese teacher, Miss Simpson, passes by and I ask her if she would give me some help writing business letters in Japanese. She's a bit taken aback. When she agrees, Vince openly sniggers. I chase after him.

'And what are you sniggering at?'

'Get a life!'

'*You* get a life! What's your problem? Don't you think I can write letters in Japanese?'

Vince does the Monopoly look again. It's halfway between a triumphant smile and a vicious sneer. He stares at me.

'No.'

'Oh yeah? Yeah?'

'Emily, we did six months of Japanese! All we learnt was how to order a cheap lunch!'

That's it. I'll show him. Bloody Vince. I'll show him who can succeed in business. Loser. And I'll hang around with the Cools, if they'll have me. I will become a Grade A Cool. I will become more cool than Cool. I bellow 'Loser!'

But I'm upset. I'm upset through the rest of school. I'm upset on the ferry. As we draw into the island, I notice Clem crashing up through the swamp.

'Em! Blanche says John's leaving!'

'What!'

'They had this terrible fight! John wants to find some other firm to buy the kelp!'

As we get to the factory, crowds are

milling anxiously. Blanche is striding among them with a triumphant smile.

'He won't be back. I told him. We don't want any of his French nonsense here, thank you very much . . .'

'Look at the big wave!'

It's Cinnamon, Tiff's eldest. She's five and she's got new glasses. Nobody takes any notice. But a whole group of children start to shout out the same thing.

'Look at the big wave! Look at the big wave!'

We look. It's not a big wave. Well, it is a big wave, but what's making the big wave is a huge power boat.

It's being driven by John.

Chapter 14

John roars up to the jetty. He leaps off and ties up the boat. It's white, gleaming and magnificent. So's he.

'Three cheers for John!'

It's Clem ... who else.

'Hip hip hooray! Hip hip hooray! Hip hip hooray!'

John puts up a hand to stop the chorus of 'For He's a Jolly Good Fellow'.

'All hands to the mill! Office equipment!'

The family surges towards the boat. John hands out box after box. There is a computer, a printer, a fax machine with a built-in answering machine, paper, box files, computer discs ... They get passed in a human chain all the way up to the house. John comes up to Blanche with a large box of chocolates.

'Here, Blanche. No hard feelings, I hope.'

Blanche throws back her head. She looks at the chocolates as if they're poison.

'If you enter that office ever again, I will resign and find work elsewhere.'

Blanche, you idiot!

John's smile tightens. 'Fine. Resignation accepted.'

He beams at me and plonks the chocolates in my hands.

'Here, Em, grab these and come and help me set up the computer!'

'Emily,' Blanche says, 'I forbid you to help that man!'

There's a sudden silence. I gulp. John glances at us both then raises his eyebrows and walks off. He's letting me decide. I'm terrified.

'But Mum . . .'

'Don't you "Mum" me! That man is trying to ruin us!'

'He's trying to make us rich!'

'He's making himself rich! He's bankrupting us! Look at all these machines!'

'It's office equipment! We need it and it's tax deductible!'

'I'll "tax deduct" you!' Blanche pauses. 'Look, Emily, I don't want to hurt your feelings, but you must be able to see that John is manipulating you!'

I feel a stab of panic. Then anger.

'Why? Because he's nice to me?'

'Could it be he's nice to you for a reason? Could it be that he wants your vote?'

'No!'

'Your ten per cent!'

'No, he wouldn't do that!'

I hate her because I'm afraid. What if she's right? What if John despises me? What if the only people who like me are Blanche and Vince? Vince who's so mean and boring and who was my only friend?

I realise that without John I have nothing. That the world is this huge, empty place of hopeless despair. I am skinny, ugly Emily with crooked teeth and John is laughing at me behind my back.

I run. I run off up the beach, past Col and Clem, past the seals, past the aunties hanging kelp. I scream like I used to. But it doesn't help. My throat is aching with the need to cry. I drop on to the sand and I sob. I realise I really wanted to be at the dance. I really wanted to be part of it. And I'm not. I won't ever be.

'Emily?'

It's John.

'Go away.'

'What's wrong?'

The surf crashes. What is wrong? Everything. The way I look. The person I am. The place where I live—and will continue to for the years stretching ahead. Years and years. And I'll never be happy. I'll always be alone.

'Em?'

'John . . . are you here to rip us off?'

'No.'

I stare at him, trying to read him. He smiles.

'I mean, I s'pose if I *were* I wouldn't tell you, would I, but no, actually I'm here because . . .'

He stops. I look up at him. He's miles away, frowning.

'If I'm honest, I'm here because my marriage broke up and I needed some time away.'

What do I say? I feel rotten to have doubted him. I hate his wife, but I'm glad she's gone. He came to me. John's smiling wistfully.

'You're thinking about your wife.'

'Mm? Oh no. I was thinking what a

god-awful pong those seals give off. How do you stand it?'

'We don't.'

John puts a matey arm around my shoulder. I wish it was less matey.

'Come on, what can cheer you up? Would you like a pizza?'

'I'm okay . . .'

'Would you like to go to a movie?'

'Honestly . . .'

'I know!' He's triumphant. 'We'll go to the school dance!'

'But I haven't got anything to wear . . .'

'We'll buy you something.'

He's bundling me along.

'But I can't dance . . .'

'Oh rubbish. All you have to do is get up and throw yourself about. That's unless there are some strange Australian dances I don't know about.'

I giggle. Clem comes out of the boatshed with a paintbrush. He's got so much paint all over him you wonder how much got on the boats.

'Clem, tell Blanche I'm chaperoning young Emily to the school dance.'

Clem salutes. I giggle more. John salutes back and winks. My giggles go totally hysterical. He's gorgeous.

We get into the boat and roar off to the mainland.

It is the best night of my life. John talks his way into a formal dress hire shop just as they're closing. He hires a white evening suit for himself and an amazing blue dress for me, with matching shoes. He sweet-talks the lady into making my face up and doing my hair. I look so glamorous I feel a fool. I shuffle out of the cubicle.

'Hey, you look lovely!' John exclaims. 'But don't slouch like that!'

I giggle. 'I'm not . . . !'

'You're like a sack of potatoes! Stand straight! Emit confidence! First rule of business. If you *carry* yourself as if you're not worth knowing, people will *believe* you're not worth knowing! Stand straight and emit confidence!'

I walk out as straight as a sergeant major. John hails a taxi. He opens the door for me. We sail into the school grounds. As John is paying the taxi, I remove my plate and stick it in my pocket.

We sweep into the school hall like two film stars going to the Academy Awards. It's really like being in an old movie—

especially since I've taken off my glasses so everything's blurred. Every head in the place turns and every girl is dying of jealousy. Mrs Mills' eyebrows shoot up into her fringe and stay there all night. Vince's scowl is very rewarding. I watch John charm everybody but him and I'm smiling so hard my face hurts. It strikes me that an-hour-and-a-half ago I wanted to die. Ah well ... My life seems a bit like that at the moment.

John dances brilliantly. I kind of bob at the knees and dangle my arms.

Some slow music starts. *What if John puts his arms around me*! I nearly die of ecstasy at the thought.

But he doesn't. He grins and says, 'Phew! I'm knackered! Fancy a Coke?'

He buys Fantas for practically the whole of Year Nine. Justin keeps standing next to me and ogling my blue dress. It makes me nervous so I crack jokes. Justin *smiles*. It's a bit chilling.

We get home after midnight. As I'm sitting on my bed, beaming, thinking about it all, there's a knock at my door. It's Blanche. She's awkward.

'Look, I'm sorry about earlier. I didn't mean to hurt your feelings.'

I'm so happy I run across and hug her.

'Just give him a chance, Mum! He's got such fantastic plans!'

She stares at me.

'Emily, does this mean you're siding with him?'

I'm so ecstatic I'm not even scared.

'Mum, it's not a matter of taking sides . . . !'

'So you are.'

I don't know what to say. She leaves. I feel a flash of guilt. But then I think of John and I dance round the room with Mr Murdoch's scrapbook because I know he would be happy for me.

The first time John Tate noticed Emily's amazing beauty was when he took her to a school dance when she was only fourteen . . .

Get real! John and me! I'm even making myself blush. Still, who can tell . . .

Mr Rupert Murdoch
News Limited
United States of America

Dear Mr Murdoch,

I'm writing to inform you that my
second cousin John and I have decided
to get married . . .

I stare at the words. I smile. I rip the paper
into little pieces.
John, John, John, John, John . . .

Chapter 15

The day after the dance is Saturday. I sleep in. I wake up feeling happy without knowing why. Then I remember the dance. If my dress wasn't hanging over the chair, I'd think it was all a dream.

I drift out in my dressing gown to dream over cornflakes. Tiff's there, making instant porridge for the kids.

I crunch away. I have this urge to talk about John.

'Is John up yet?' I ask.

'Oh yes, hours ago,' Tiff replies. 'He went to the mainland.'

'What for?'

'He had a filling come out when he was eating his bacon. Blanche fixed up an appointment for him with Rod.'

I nearly choke. Blanche wouldn't dare!

Would she ever!

'Tiff, when did he go?'

'Oh, about an hour ago . . .'

I leap up from the table. Suddenly I remember Lo-Lo. She's starting her work experience today! It's terrible to be so dependent on the world's greatest walking disaster, but I've got no choice.

I ring Rod's surgery. At the other end the receiver is picked up. There is a clatter as it is dropped. Oh no . . .

'Lo, is that you? It's Emily!'

'Oh hello Em, I just dropped the phone . . .'

'Lo, has a man called John Tate come in for an appointment?'

'Is that the appointment Auntie Blanche booked?'

'Yes.'

'Ummm . . .'

I can hear Lo flicking through the appointment book.

'Yes. He's in the surgery now.'

'Oh no!'

I hang up. I have to get there. I chuck on some clothes and run to the beach. I leap into Grandpa's old motor boat and roar off. I get drenched by spray. It takes forever to get to the mainland. Finally, I

106

get there. I tie up and run. I run like a maniac. As I get into the shopping mall, my stomach turns with panic. There is John!

'John, are you all right?'

'Emily, what on earth's the matter? You're soaked ...'

'John, what did Rod do to your teeth?'

'Rod? It wasn't a Rod. It was a woman, Vicki.'

'And she didn't suggest you needed your gums fixed?'

John's amused and puzzled.

'No. But she *did* give me a collection of sticks and some salt ...'

He smiles and I scan his teeth. They look intact. I breathe a sigh of relief. Trust Lo to get it wrong.

'I must say I prefer a decent plastic brush myself, but according to Vicki if I don't use sticks I'll lose all my teeth.'

He doesn't know how close he's already got to losing all his teeth. I don't mention it.

John takes me for coffee in the poshest cafe in town. It's called 'Ziggy's'. I have an iced chocolate with about half a metre of cream swirled on top. We sit at an outside table. Crowds of people walk past.

You can tell by the glasses that most of them are Tates. John's wearing shorts and reading *Business Review Weekly*. I sneak looks at his gorgeous legs and cute, stumpy toes peering out of his sandals. I'm working out how to get the last drop out of my glass without sounding like the bathwater draining, when I see an extraordinary sight.

Across the shopping mall is Blanche. She is wheeling five supermarket trolleys locked together. She is in a bright red apron. There is a little paper hat balanced on top of the red dandelion-clock hair. She has kept her promise! She's got a job at the Supa Market! Has she given up? This is about as likely as a piranha turning vegetarian, but I can't bring myself to worry. Not with iced chocolate and John's toes.

John's party is held on Sunday on the South Beach outside the factory. Of course, it's a triumph. For a start we can all relax because Blanche is at work. Then there's the marvellous food—all brought from the mainland by a caterer.

John moves among the crowds, greeting and being greeted. Every girl flirts with him like crazy. People talk about him as if he's a saint. Saint John of the kelp. I look at the happy people, the newly painted factory gleaming in the sun. How can things have changed so quickly and so much for the better? It's just like my daydream about the young investor who lets me run the factory. Except more exciting.

The party goes on all day. Auntie Ruby plays Frank Sinatra's greatest hits on her piano accordion. As the sun sets, Clem brings out his rock'n'roll tapes. I get three dances with John. The rest of the time he's whirling aunties and cousins around and waltzing with little kids balanced on his shoes. There's this strange moment when one of the toddlers collides with a tray of cutlery. As John bends over to help pick up the stuff I notice a little bald patch on the back of his head. I'm surprised. John going bald?

But on second thoughts—I like it! I realise I like everything about him. He has changed my life. He has led me into adventure . . .

Chapter 16

The Monday after the dance, I'm still glowing. The only down side is that of course, Vince and I are still not talking. As I get on the bus, I see he's put his bag on the seat next to him. He couldn't make himself clearer. I'm planning to chicken-wing past him. But Justin, in the front seat, puts an arm out and grunts. He indicates a free seat next to him!

The whole bus is watching—except Vince, who is the picture of a sulk. That settles it. I sit next to Justin. The bus gasps. I am now officially a Cool and everyone is amazed.

That includes me. Is it because of the blue dress? Is it because the cools think John has brought money into my family? Or is it that I'm some kind of entertainment? Maybe Justin is getting bored on the deadpan planet of Cool. I half close my eyes. I let my mouth hang open. Emily, the ultimate Cool ...

We stop at the traffic lights where there is a poster of Yarradindi Doug preferring his glass of beer to a Greek statue. The bald old man with chest-high shorts is arguing with a little old lady. It's about her geriatric dog, which is off the lead. The dog stands there panting desperately. Its eyes move from one to the other. It's concentrating on not collapsing. Justin leans out of the window. He shouts, 'Oi, nincompoop!' The old man shakes his fist. The Cools and I cheer.

As we get off the bus, Justin is at my side. I realise I am officially sitting next to him from now on. In English we've started studying world mythology. We're up to the Golden Fleece—which is about a magic ram with golden wool that flies around rescuing kids. Mr Bergonzi says it's no sillier than Superman and at the time was as popular as *Home and Away*. I whisper to Justin that the ram was probably a great surfer as well. Justin giggles and tells all the Cools. All the Cools giggle. Justin asks Mr Bergonzi whether the ram was a great surfer as well. Mr Bergonzi gives him a detention.

At lunchtime I get involved with Lies for the first time. Lies is Justin's heavy metal rock group. There are four of them. Jason and Kylie Wallop play guitars, a girl called Sophie (with blue dreadlocks) plays drums, and a boy who has never been known to utter a word plays keyboard.

Lies never play any gigs. In fact, they don't seem to be able to play one complete song. They can do half of quite a lot of songs really well. But then someone makes a mistake. By the time they've had a fight about who it was and everyone's threatened to go off in a huff, the only way to continue is by starting another song.

Lies exists to torment Mr Thompson. Mr Thompson is the music teacher. He's a small, old man with sloping shoulders whose big mistake was to try to make music interesting. He started off by showing us videos of musicals, but people got bored.

So when Ben Traversi accidentally got a Tic Tac mint stuck in his ear in the middle of *West Side Story* and had to be taken to casualty, kids started copying him. Three people were taken out of *The King and I*. Finally, the whole class got put on detention when Sophie (the Cool with blue dreadlocks) tried to push a Mintie up one nostril and gave herself a nosebleed.

So Mr Thompson decided to give us a project. He split the whole of Year Eight up into groups and got each one to do a study on their favourite kind of music. This was going quite well until trouble broke out between the country and western fans and the metalheads.

The problem was that the metalheads have to be aggressive and shout insulting remarks. It's part of the metal thing. And even though metal lyrics are all about death and torture and revenge, most metal fans are usually quite weedy under the leather. Country and western fans, on the other hand, tend to be built like brick dunnies.

Anyway, there was a big fight next to the basketball courts and Jennifer Bates, who was going to do a tribute to Kylie Minogue, got her flute bent. Mr Thompson intervened to save Justin and the metal heads from head injuries.

Justin has never forgiven him. In revenge, Justin formed Lies. Every school music evening Lies swaggers on stage to accompany the school band in playing patriotic hits. It takes them twenty minutes to tune up amid bloodcurdling whistles of feedback. They don't actually play. They stand there squinting at the music and raising their eyebrows at the thought of being expected to play such garbage. Meanwhile the band shrieks and bashes its way through 'I Still Call Australia Home'.

This time Lies is getting ready for the parents and teachers' evening. They are playing a song written by Sophie called 'Lover'. Justin and I walk into the music room.

Poor Mr Thompson is sitting on a chair at the back. He looks weary but he drags a smile across his face.

'Morning, Justin!' Mr Thompson looks a bit surprised to see me there, but smiles. I chicken-wing to an empty seat and loll on it with my mouth half open. Mr Thompson suggests we get started.

He's grimly bright and cheerful. He knows they're out to get him. The band members look at each other. They smile dangerously. They start to play. It's deafening. It's terrible. It takes about ten minutes to get

to the lyrics, but when they come, they get
repeated over and over again.

> I lurve your face.
> I lurve your lips.
> I wanna stick my tongue
> Into your armpits ...

The smile doesn't shift from Mr Thompson's face. The song continues.

> I lurve your heart.
> I lurve your soul.
> I lick the hairs that sprout
> Outa your moles.

Justin, more active than I've ever seen him,
writhes over the desks and tosses chalk
around between rifts.

The whole thing finishes with a typical
ear-shattering whine of feedback and a
huge battering on the drums. They turn
triumphantly to Mr Thompson.

'Very nice. I'll put it on after the Year
Seven recorder band.'

'D'ya see his face!'

'Yeah! He was ropeable!'

We're behind the toilets. This is Cool territory. The bell's about to go, so Justin, Kylie and Sophie aren't actually smoking. Mind you, the smell of cigarette smoke is so strong you could probably get cancer just by sniffing the bricks. They're celebrating their victory over Mr Thompson.

I think it was Mr Thompson's victory, but I don't say. I join in the laughter. I feel a bit weird being with them, but it's amazing the respect you get.

Vince walks past. He looks at me and sneers. I look back and sneer. Justin calls out, 'Yay!' The Cools pack up with loud nasal sniggers. Jason adds, 'Go nerd! What's that stink of seaweed!' By this time the Cools are nearly splitting their sides. Dylan Pocky, who's only a probationary Cool, does his weird, high-pitched giggle and chucks an empty chocolate milk carton after Vince.

The bell goes. I instinctively start for the classrooms, but Justin puts his hand on my arm. Five minutes later we stroll across. We make an entrance. Boy do we make an entrance ...

We throw open the door. We stand frozen for an instant, heads tipped to one side, just long enough to get the teacher seething but not long enough to get a detention. Then—I realise I've been dying to do this all my life—we shuffle in dragging our feet and slouching our shoulders. I chicken-wing in slow motion. It stops the entire class.

Miss Henderson takes a long menacing drag of breath, then realises that if she puts us in detention she'll have to stay behind as well. We flop insolently into our seats. It's the high point of the Cool day.

Ms Emily Tate
Tate Island
Victoria
Australia

Dear Ms Tate,

Mr Murdoch thanks you for your kind letter and wishes you every success in your chosen career.

Yours sincerely,

F W Paterson

For and on behalf of
Rupert Murdoch

Chapter 17

Over the next week I find myself spending more and more time with the Cools. We don't do much. Mostly we hang around the back of the toilets coughing. Cigarettes are expensive, so we make do by giving chest-splitting, shoulder-hunching smoker's coughs every time anyone walks past. The boys spit. Kylie does the back of Sophie's hair. Meanwhile, Sophie selects hairs from her fringe and sets them alight with a plastic cigarette lighter. We gather round to watch them frizzle.

A few times we go out to the shopping mall at lunchtime. Usually, the point of this is to watch Dylan Pocky run out from behind the new federation-style bandstand and shout 'Dur!' at passers-by. One day an old lady hits him in the stomach with her handbag. He's winded, but he shouts 'Dur!' again. So she hits him again. Another time, Justin needs to pick up some antibiotic cream for an infected nose-ring hole. While we're at the chemist's, Justin has another hole pierced in his eyebrow. If he gets any more little rings on his eyebrows he'll be able to run a curtain rail between them.

The Cools spend a lot of time watching Dylan perform mindless acts of self-punishment. We watch Dylan jumping off the railway bridge into the river. We watch Dylan leaping in front of cars. We watch Dylan balancing bricks on his head. I think for Dylan, it's a family thing. Particularly the head injuries. His Dad, Terry, is famous in Yarradindi for being able to stop overhead fans by bringing his head slowly into contact with the centre bit beneath the blades. Terry Pocky has waist-length blond hair. As well as the fan trick, he's famous for swallowing lighted cigarettes and racing stock cars at the weekend. He runs his own rubbish removal service. His truck's got SATAN'S ANGEL and some red and orange flames painted on the door. He also acts as bouncer at the Bowling Club.

A week with the Cools is a long time. I hate to say it but I'm missing Vince. I know he's missing me. In science, he has to do experiments on his own so it takes twice the time and the teacher bellows at him. The same thing happens in Home Studies. He gets left the crummy cooker. While he's frantically writing up the recipes, his Tomato Chicken goes dry and his custard boils over. He glares at me.

Of course, now I'm a Cool, I don't even do experiments or cooking because I'm not trusted with fire, but Vince still steams. The trouble is, the Cools don't understand my jokes. And I don't really understand theirs. I thought for ages we were laughing at Dylan Pocky because he was such a moron. Now I realise we're laughing at him because of his sophisticated wit.

But there is always John to daydream about. When the Cools bore me rigid, I just tune out. And going home at nights is one surprise after another. For a start, instead of going ballistic with revenge after John escaped getting his gums ripped open, Blanche has simply developed a strangely peaceful smile and started eating in her room. She is clearly plotting something, but I don't have time to puzzle out what because the island is changing by the minute. It starts with the painting. Col and Clem are set loose with paintbrushes and huge cans of white paint. They paint from morning to night. First they paint the inside walls of the factory, three times. Then they paint the outside. When they see how pleased John is, they start to paint everything in sight. They paint the roof and all the sheds. They paint all the rowing boats. They paint the jetty. They paint the chook pen (various dumb chooks are stalking around splattered with paint). They paint the lines where we dry the kelp (including the ropes, which have to be replaced because the paint comes off).

To make up for that mistake, they paint the rocks next to the paths. When John's pleased with that, they paint the paths. As you approach the island its whiteness is dazzling. I have this vision that one day I'll come home and see the mangrove swamps and the mud painted white, but John tactfully stops them before it gets to this. He reassigns them to demolition.

This is a terrifying sight. Col and Clem are instructed to bash a large doorway in the factory wall so a drying and packing room can be added on. This is part of John's plan to help us sell the dried kelp to other people. They each have a huge hammer and take it in turns to swing and crack at the brick walls. Dust flies. The wall snaps like biscuit. Col and Clem's big moon faces are bright red and streaming with sweat. Their arms are bright green and streaming with sweat.

John has a seaweed expert and a Government Health Inspector touring the island so we can get our licence to produce foodstuffs. As John and the visitors approach, Clem and Col have stopped— for the first time all afternoon—to let the aunties stroll by with washing baskets of kelp. Col sees the experts coming and he frets. He doesn't want to be seen not doing anything. He shouts at the aunties to hurry up. They shout back. Finally, he's so anxious that he gives the wall an almighty whack before the aunties are completely clear.

John and the visitors round the corner just in time to see a clump of broken bricks as big as a Christmas turkey flying through the air towards the retreating aunties. They scream a warning, the aunties duck, and the clump comes hurtling on towards *them*!

Everyone screams. The clump lands harmlessly on the sand like a fallen meteor. Everyone breathes a sigh of relief. The Health Inspector makes a joke. Then stubs his toe on a kelp hook.

The next day, two men from the mainland install a prefabricated shed next to Col and Clem's hole in the wall. As soon as we get our kelp-drying kiln, this will become the drying and packing room. Once the kiln is installed, we will be able to dry huge amounts of kelp.

This is truly a techonological miracle, but there is a hitch. Drying has always been the aunties' job, so it's logical for John to make them all dryers and packers. So he calls a meeting and explains what's about to happen when we get the kiln installed.

What John doesn't realise is that the aunties' pecking order—who's boss—has been developed over a century and it depends on so many crazy details that it's like a secret society. The boss is Auntie Vi. But who comes next in the pecking order depends on more than just age, or how closely they are related to Grandpa.

It also depends on how Vi is feeling. In particular, it depends on whether she won at bingo this week. Bingo is held every Friday in the caravan park barbecue area. If Auntie Vi has won a few games, she is kindness itself. If she has lost, she is ratty. If she has lost to any of the other aunties, the drying and collecting process is misery for all concerned.

But John's not aware of any of this. So one day when I'm not there, he tells Auntie Glad—the baby—that she will be first in the line. He tells Auntie Dot that she will be last. What's more, he tells the others (*including Auntie Vi!*) to fit themselves in where they like. This is a bit like ordering Attila the Hun to go and put on the kettle. Of course, Auntie Vi would never stoop so low as to *tell* John she has to be boss, and the others are afraid to.

I get home to find all the aunties sitting in their armchairs outside the plant claiming to be ill. Auntie Vi's face is like thunder. I pick the problem immediately, but a solution's tricky. We have to please Auntie Vi, but also keep Auntie Glad happy.

I suggest Auntie Glad is kept first in line,

but Auntie Vi is made Supervisor. Her job is to stride about holding a clipboard. Everyone's pleased. John slaps me on the back. It's so nice to be appreciated. I glow.

I'm glowing a lot these days. Every night John and I talk business. It's bliss. It's just like Emily of Emily Enterprises, except I'm not wearing shoulder pads. John has finally got through to Yarradindi Beers. They are going to pay us all the money they owe us. John is going to make them pay more for it next time.

Sometimes we stroll along the beach (John's installed a fence to give us a stretch of seal-free sand). We talk about my idea for a kelp-based face pack. John's getting his experts to look into it. We talk about profit and loss, investments, the money market. John is teaching me accounting. I tell him about a boarding school that gives you an education in commerce. I bring home versions of business letters in Japanese that I copied from a book in the library for us to adapt.

Everything is going wonderfully. Even Blanche looks benign. Then John gets news that Bobbly Brains kelp is not only edible, but top quality and a Japanese company are extremely interested in buying it. He tells the assembled family that he is hoping to get the Japanese company to come into partnership with us. They will provide the money to buy the packing and processing equipment. We will provide the kelp and the workers. Then, as soon as our food-manufacturing licence is through, we will start to pack and export kelp as food. Everyone cheers, including Blanche! *Who shakes John's hand*! Could she have given up? I mean, it's possible. With John, anything's possible. I feel a great wave of affection for her. Good old Blanche . . .

Then one recess, two Year Sevens come pounding up.

'Are you Emily Tate? Your cousin John's in trouble!'

My stomach turns in panic. I look to where they are pointing.

Oh no . . .

Lo-Lo, sobbing, is clinging to the wire fence of the basketball courts.

I hurry across to her.

'Lo, what's the matter?'

'Oh Em, it's John Tate.'

'Yes?'

'Rod's sawing his gums up this afternoon.'

Chapter 18

I'm stunned. I'm angry! I'm very angry!
I'm going to rip Blanche limb from limb!
No wonder she looked smug!

'I mean, he's so old, Em, his records
say he's seventy-five.'

Wait a minute ...

'Lo, this is very important. Does John
Tate *look* seventy-five?'

'Well, Em, I don't know. He could
have been seventy-four. Or he could have
been older than seventy-five, he could
have been eighty ... Then again, Auntie
Vi's only sixty-five and ...'

I bellow, 'Is John Tate an old man?'

Lo's eyes widen and she stammers.

'Yes, Em. At least, *old* Mr John Tate
is an old man. *Young* Mr John Tate isn't.

He's cute, young Mr John Tate. Hasn't he got fantastic legs . . .'

It turns out that Lo got confused on the day John got his tooth fixed. Rod told her to expect an old man. Perhaps Blanche hadn't told him that old Uncle John was dead. Perhaps Rod had been so dazzled that he didn't listen. It doesn't really matter. What happened was that Lo mistook some poor old man for John. When the real John came in she just thought he was yet another Tate. After all, Yarradindi's full of us. So, while the real John had his filling fixed, Rod told the poor old man that his gums had to be carved into flaps. And the appointment to have it done is today.

When I explain to her what she's done, Lo goes pale, her eyes pop and her left leg starts shaking. When Lo's left leg starts shaking you've got approximately twenty seconds before she screams and faints. Within fifteen seconds a prefect and I have got her to the drinking fountain. Lo turns it on. The tap comes off in her hand and a huge jet of water flies up and soaks the entire descant section of the Year Seven recorder band, who happen to be gathering to perform in Assembly.

'Lo, you have to tell Rod!'

'How can I? He'll kill me! And the Principal'll kill me! I mean, Em, s'posing I've got other people muddled up! S'posing everyone's had the wrong thing done to them!'

Lo's left leg starts shaking again. I know it's madness to get involved with one of poor Lo's disasters, but after all, it is my mother who started it.

'Lo, have you any idea who this old man is?'

'No!'

I've got ten seconds.

'Lo, would anyone who was in the waiting room know who he was?'

'There wasn't anybody!'

Five seconds. Lo's getting paler, and now the other leg is shaking . . .

'Lo, did he mention an address?'

Lo suddenly beams.

'Yes! Yes, Em! He wrote his address!'

Lo's so relieved she steps backwards and treads on a Year Eight's banana.

She says, 'Sorry.'

I swing into action at lunchtime. I am to meet Lo in the mall and get the address. Luckily, the others won't miss me because they are going down to watch Dylan

Pocky bang his head against the plate-glass window of the new Hot Bread shop. It's got a sticker on it saying it's bullet-proof, so Dylan needs to try it out. I'll just slip away when no-one is looking. To be honest, I'm quite glad to be getting away. Justin keeps trying to take my hand.

And the most appalling thing is that I think any minute now I'm supposed to kiss Justin. The last time I kissed Justin was when I was five, it was a dare, and he punched me in the kidneys. Now I find myself thinking I might need to punch him in the kidneys.

Anyway, the time is definitely getting close because a couple of days ago when we were in the mall, he bought a huge aerosol can of Brut deodorant. By the amount he's using, I think he must spray it up in the air every morning and run underneath. The bus reeks. I'm taking no chances. I avoid being alone with Justin.

I sneak off as Dylan is gearing himself for his first run at the window. My plan is to tell the old man that Rod is having a nervous breakdown and he should get another dentist. Which, actually, is not far from the truth.

I meet Lo outside the Fast Foto shop.

The address is great because it backs on to the mall, so I should be able to get back to school in time. I run over there. It's a lovely little house with a beautiful garden. An apple-cheeked old lady is pruning the bushes.

I walk up to her and ask, 'Excuse me, does an elderly gentleman live here?'

'My husband Neville does. Why, dear?'

I am just about to reply when there's screaming and whooping and smacking of shoes on the footpath. The entire gang of Cools comes pounding out of a sidestreet where they've managed to lose the security guard who was chasing them. They're jubilant. Dylan chucks himself at a passing car in triumph.

'Yay, Emily!'

'Where ya going, Emily?'

At this moment, an elderly man comes limping out from the house towards the old lady. He is carrying a whipper snipper. He wears shorts that come up to his chest. I look at him. My smile freezes on my face.

Neville is the bossy old man! He sees the Cools and me. He lets out a terrible bellow of rage. He turns on the whipper snipper, holds it aloft like a buzzing spear, and comes charging lopsidedly towards us roaring, 'Nincompoops!'

The man is demented. He's trying to scalp us. We run. Dylan runs round in circles shouting 'Dur!' for a few seconds, but even he realises that Neville won't be stopped.

We meet up under the bridge, all panting. Justin flops on to the ground and Sophie goes into a racking cough that's for real. Kylie's mascara has run wildly and she looks like a panda. But Dylan's beaming. He keeps saying, 'Oh *yeah*! Oh *yeah*!'

I catch him looking at me. There's a strange light in his eye. Then, impulsively, he whips up his T-shirt to reveal his scrawny, brown-lined stomach. He's staring at me. He snarls, 'Punch this!'

Everyone looks up in surprise. I'm horrified. This is love.

We get back to school just before the bell. I rush to the payphone and ring Rod's surgery.

'Lo, you've got to own up! I couldn't stop him!'

But Lo's delirious with happiness.

'Rod didn't do it! He made me ring up and cancel the appointment!'

I breathe a sigh of relief. I should have guessed Rod wouldn't be able to go through with it. But we're not out of the woods yet.

'Lo, you have to promise me you'll tell.'

There is a silence. I can imagine Lo's left leg starting.

I shout, 'Lo?'

I hear the phone drop. She's gone. I sigh. I suppose I'll have to tell Rod. Then it occurs to me that if I do I put John in danger. This is insane.

I lean my head wearily against the wall. A lump of chewing gum sticks to my hair. Just as I'm trying to untangle it, I see Miss Simpson coming along the corridor. I suddenly remember John's talk about the Japanese company that's interested in our kelp. I call out, 'Miss Simpson, you know those business letters you helped me write, well . . .'

Miss Simpson interrupts me. She beams.

'Yes, isn't it wonderful that you're going to process the seaweed for food!

John was telling me. And guess what, I'm coming to the island to do all your translations for you! Now *that* will save you a job, won't it, Emily!'

I'm stunned.

Chapter 19

On the bus home I sit next to Jennifer
Bates and close my eyes. My life is a nightmare. I've gone from being the class dag
to being pursued by the two people in the
class most likely to become serial killers.
And on top of all that, John doesn't think
I'm capable of writing business letters.

Jennifer shows me her fossil of a snail.
She rattles on about her flute exam and
some female saxophone player in Sydney
who does concerts in the nude for art. I'm
glad Lies hasn't heard about this because
I think Mr Thompson has enough to put
up with. Justin and Dylan peer at me sus-
piciously from separate sides of the bus. I
pretend not to be looking. I check them
out in the reflection in the bus window.
Vince's mouth looks like a cat's bottom.

When I get home I don't want to talk to John. I am disgusted with him. He knocks at my door.

'Em.'

'Go away.'

'Look, are you upset about me getting Miss Simpson to do the translations?'

'No.'

'The point is, every time I ask you to compose a letter, you have to take it to Miss Simpson to be checked. It adds an extra day. Time is money, Em, don't go grouchy on me now.'

I'm weakening. I hear him sigh. I imagine his frown. I suddenly realise that being upset has nothing to do with business. It has to do with John seeing a lot of Miss Simpson, who's heavy-featured and plump up the top but has fantastic legs. She reminds me of those books with pages cut into three where you make weird-looking people by combining different legs, heads and bodies. Miss Simpson's got a freckly, ordinary face and a body like two prize pumpkins on top of each other. But the legs sticking out underneath belong to some Hollywood sex queen.

Miss Simpson seems to realise this because she goes in for a lot of colourful tights and striding leg movements and always acts as lifesaver at the swimming carnival. She once pretended she was saving Vince from drowning in the Under Twelves' Butterfly, but everybody knew she just wanted to dive in in front of the Area Education Co-ordinator. She spent most of the day flying off the end of the springboard and dragging out protesting kids.

'Em? Look, I value your help enormously, but you, of all people, wouldn't put some personal thing ahead of the business, would you?'

I would. If I could. But how can I stop him liking Miss Simpson if he wants to? I feel shut out. I want to cry. I feel myself plummeting down. What do I have without John? Lies? Dylan Pocky? Kissing Justin in a suffocating cloud of Brut? I get a vision of Miss Simpson's freckly face as she teaches us to order coffee cake. Her lips writhe about around the vowels as she does this fake Japanese voice.

She once told us she stayed with a Japanese family and everybody, including the grandad, got in the bath together. They must have got a shock.

John says sadly, 'Em, really. Don't take offence. Please.'

I know Miss Simpson's rainbow tights will be leaping through my nightmares, but I can't resist him. As I open the door he holds out a paper bag and grins.

'Peace offering. Macadamia nuts. I've just discovered them. Aren't they brilliant?'

We walk along the beach chomping nuts and talking about the money market.

Half an hour later, John's gone to phone Miss Simpson and I'm starting on a mountain of ironing that Tiff has been moving around for a month. Blanche walks in. She's trying to stop smiling. She says solemnly, 'I'm sorry, but it had to be done. Today, Emily . . .' She pauses theatrically, 'Today Rod started surgery on John's gums, surgery which will make him unable to speak for three days.'

At that very moment John walks in tossing a handful of nuts into his mouth.

'Hello, Blanche. Fancy a few macadamias?'

Blanche is hissing fiercely down the phone. She's winding the phone cord round and round as if she's going to strangle someone with it. I imagine poor old Rod at the other end, one hairy earhole pressed to the earpiece.

'Sorry for him? This man is going to destroy us! He's already sweet-talked Emily and Tiff. He's bought off the islanders with a crummy party! And there isn't a woman working in Supa Market who isn't going on about how *handsome* he is and what *wonderful legs* he's got and what wonderful sexy clothes he wears ...'

I can imagine Rod's a bit puzzled at the idea of Neville being a spunk. Neville's legs are skinny and covered in veins. This, combined with the weird effect of his chest-high shorts, is definitely not sexy.

Blanche listens irritably then bellows, 'Stop making excuses and think of something!'

As she hangs up, Tiff ambles by with a twin under each arm.

'Was that Rod? He's such a nice man.' She giggles. 'D'you know he gave Stevie two toothbrushes?'

I gasp.

Oh Tiff! Rod is Blanche's property!

But Blanche doesn't notice. She's plotting.

I leave them to it. I finish the ironing, tell the twins a bedtime story, and walk outside to the beach. Ah, John. The island is so unbelievably neat! The buildings gleam with white paint. The higgledy-piggledy kelp-drying lines have gone. The boats are all moored in a line. In the distance, the aunties stride about in the lab coats that John bought them.

I need to tell Mr Murdoch.

Mr Rupert Murdoch
News Limited
United States of America

Dear Mr Murdoch,

This is to inform you that the first stage of our remodelling is completed and ready for your inspection.

Yours sincerely,

Emily Tate

Chapter 20

I have this terrible dream that Justin and Dylan are burning the place down while Miss Simpson and John dance cheek-to-cheek on the verandah. I wake up to discover that Tiff is cooking John breakfast. John must have a stomach like steel. As I join him at the table for my cornflakes, he's tucking into burnt bacon and greasy black fried eggs. Tiff is fluttering around in her kimono. Cinnamon has a floppy bit of toast. The twins sit dripping baby food. They cling to the tables of their highchairs with sticky little hands as if they're about to drive them away. They give off that weird biscuity smell that small kids have.

John turns to me as I'm taking out my plate. These days I place it in a glass of water for meals. I've decided this is the least antisocial way of handling the problem. I always do it with my little finger crooked.

'Morning Em, you need to be in on this. I want to build a new plant.'

I'm stunned.

'What? Completely new?'

'I've been doing some homework. By the time we pour in thousands trying to make the old place conform to the health regulations for food manufacturing, we might as well start from scratch. It's actually cheaper to start from scratch. We might turn the old place into a museum.'

A museum! Well, I suppose the tourists might be interested. Those with no sense of smell.

'We could put Col and Clem into historical costumes,' adds John jovially. 'The aunties could sell scones.'

'I could *make* scones!' beams Tiff.

John chuckles diplomatically. Tiff's scones would really boost the tourist trade. People could come to the island to die.

'What about the smell?' I ask.

'I don't know, yet! Perhaps we could make it a feature!'

Visit Tate Island and burn the hairs off the inside of your nostrils!

As the cornflakes scratch against my tender gums, I realise that I'm not really against the idea of a new building and a tourist attraction. I'm just annoyed because he chose to tell Tiff before me. I realise that every time John talks to another woman I'm jealous. I hate it because it's a real bore having to worry about him all the time, but I can't help it. I remember my dream. Miss Simpson was wearing a miniskirt so short you could wrap your sandwiches in it.

'So, what do you think?'

They're both looking at me. Tiff's heaping more blackened eggs onto John's plate. They cruise across his plate on a slick of black oil and slither to a halt next to his bacon rind. She's beaming.

'I think it's a wonderful idea,' she glows. 'And do you know, Em, John's getting me a housekeeper, so I can help in the office.'

I realise John has Tiff's vote anyway.

'Can we afford it?'

'Good question, Emily. We'd need a substantial investment from a partner. I think it'd pay us back in no time. But you and Tiff mustn't take my word for it. Get professional advice. Go to George . . .'

He stops, because there, standing in the doorway, is Blanche. John smiles.

'Hello, Blanche! Isn't it a beautiful morning!'

And then I gasp—because Blanche does something I haven't seen since Grandpa died. She plonks herself down at the table, whips out a pencil and pad and writes, with grim determination, 'Get nicked!'

She pushes the pad to John. He reads it and a smile twitches on his lips. He writes something in his beautiful italic script and pushes it back.

It reads, 'I will if you will!'

I mull things over as I brush my teeth and snap my plate back into position. I really need to talk to George about John's plans. As for Blanche, she is clearly on the warpath again. I dread to think what will happen when she finds out about this new plant.

I catch sight of John's toothpaste. It's the same brand as ours but all the writing's in French. His electric razor is next to it. His aftershave is something with a French name.

I'm glad he doesn't use Brut. I open the bottle so I can summon the essence of

John. I close my eyes romantically and take a long, swooning sniff. It's so incredibly chemical at first that it hits the back of my throat and makes my eyes water. But then, magically, it wafts of John. I smile dreamily. Then, for some unknown reason I have a vivid image of Miss Simpson capering about in her leopard-skin tights, sniffing. A flame of jealousy soars inside me like a bunsen burner. I catch the early ferry so I can see George. Tiff's on the ferry too, giggling about an appointment with Rod. She's wearing mascara.

Vince is still eating his breakfast when I walk in the back door. Auntie Stella smiles brightly and offers me some tea. I say no. Vince scrapes his chair back and disappears without a word.

George takes me into his office and I ask his advice. He feels that a new plant will pay for itself in a few years.

'The only problem is . . .'

He stops and frowns.

'Is John doing the best for the family? Sometimes business efficiency means putting people out of work. I wonder if he appreciates what that would do to us.'

As angry and jealous as I am about

John, I'm outraged at George's question.

'Uncle George, John's worked miracles on the island! He's going to make everyone rich! The only people who don't like him are you and Vince and Blanche! You're so mean to him!'

And I storm out. I'm ropeable. It's so unfair! Now, as far as *I'm* concerned, John can build two new plants if he wants. George's mum, Nanny Ethel, is sitting in the garden reading *Cattleman's Weekly* and eating Minties.

Nanny Eth only stays with George and Stella from time to time. She's never forgiven him for becoming a solicitor instead of mustering cattle according to family tradition. Nanny's family were famous cattle musterers, Nanny included. When Grandpa's cousin Bill married her she was working in travelling rodeo shows. She did a stockwhip act under the name of 'Ethel, Queen of the Drovers'. Her speciality was flicking lighted cigarettes out of people's mouths with the stockwhip.

Nanny's favourite comment on anything is, 'Never trust a Tate.' When you point out that she's a Tate through marriage, she denies it.

As I go past, Nanny Ethel shouts out,

'And you can tell that Pom to keep off North Beach!'

'He never goes near North Beach!' Under my breath, I add, 'You silly old coot!'

Nanny Eth is still reading. She yells, 'I heard that!'

I walk through the school gates just as the second bell is going. This is a relief. No Justin or Dylan. Then I hear a whoop from the sky above. It's not a religious experience.

It's Dylan Pocky hanging by one hand from the top branch of a Moreton Bay Fig tree. He's screeching and waving. The tree is bending and swaying. This is what courtship must have been like in the Stone Age.

He screams a bit more, then gives a yell and drops like a stone on to the asphalt. I wheel off in the opposite direction. I'm not getting stuck in an ambulance with Dylan. That's if they'd take him again. Last time, after they got him into Casualty, they found he'd drawn a man with enormous rude bits in indelible felt-tip pen on their stretcher.

He catches up to me and punches me on the arm affectionately. I punch him on the arm with malice.

'Get lost, Dylan.'

This is the worst thing to do. Dylan assumes I'm enjoying this. He rubs his arm and hoots with glee.

'Wanna arm wrestle?'

'No.'

'Go on!'

'No, Dylan! I said, get lost!'

He's circling me. He seems to have springs in his knees.

'Dur!' he says, sticking his face into mine affectionately.

'Dur!' he says, trying to pull my bag off my arm.

It all wells up. My anger at George, my jealousy about John, Blanche's madness with Neville, Vince sulking.

I let out a bloodcurdling scream. I grab the closest weapon to hand, which is my lunch box. I grab Dylan by the scruff of his neck and batter him all over the asphalt, shouting, 'Get lost! Get lost!' The lunch box splits near the bubblers and my cheese sandwich and banana go flying, but I continue.

As Dylan breaks away, laughing, I hurl

it after him. It misses, but I feel good doing it. As I stand getting my breath, I look up. I see Kylie Wallop staring at me from under her fringe like an evil Shetland pony. Her lip curls and she says, 'Bitch.'

I realise that Kylie is in love with Dylan.

Chapter 21

My life is starting to sound like a bad pop song. Everybody loves the wrong people. Even poor old Tiff's yearning after Rod. Meanwhile John, the man *I* long for (even though it's hopeless), is probably at this moment flirting wildly with Miss Simpson. Who, incidentally, turned up today wearing a clinging red leotard and a miniskirt so small it makes the sandwich wrapper she wore in my dream look gigantic. She smiled at me a lot and did a lot of Japanese greetings and bowings, which I think is supposed to be a cute way of getting into my good books so she can flirt with John. I look at my legs. Sticks. I hate Miss Simpson.

In English I sit next to Jennifer Bates, while Justin and Dylan keep staring at me.

We're up to the bit in the mythology section where Zeus, who's the king of the gods, keeps turning himself into weird things every time he sees a mortal woman he thinks is cute. Frankly, I can't see the point. You'd think he'd have a much better chance fronting up as a god than as a peacock or a parrot or a bunch of bananas, whatever it was. In fact, I'd say Zeus has a serious problem.

I think of John. He looks like a god. I wish I could turn myself into something that would appeal to him. It's hopeless. I think about the last time he put his arm around me. He's never put his arm around me properly, of course. It's always been matey, or moving me out of the way, but it's a major part of my day.

I realise he hasn't done it for days. Why? I torture myself with images of his wife turning up. Or of him marrying Miss Simpson and me being bridesmaid.

(*I smile bravely as she marches up the aisle in a long veil and a white satin mini-skirt. As they're going off on their honeymoon, I turn my tear-stained face to John (I'm not wearing my plate) and I say, 'Be happy, John. Think of me sometimes.'*)

The picture of Zeus with his hair

permed like old Mrs Hurley blurs through my tears. (Mrs Hurley takes the Catholics for Optional Religion and gives out Maltesers to those who express an interest.)

Rupert Murdoch
News Limited
United States of America

Dear Mr Murdoch,

Unfortunately, I will be unable to attend our forthcoming meeting because my partner is marrying my Japanese teacher and I will be dying of grief.

Yours sincerely,

Emily Tate

(*Rupert Murdoch strides through the kelp factory to where Emily is hunched in a corner weeping. 'My God, Emily, are you all right?' He turns to a cute-looking young businessman behind him. 'Johnson, get help. This girl has the business mind of the century. John Tate is a damned fool.*

And Johnson,' Johnson turns, 'execute Miss Simpson.')

When the bell sounds I'm out like a shot and running for the bus stop. If I hurry I can get the public bus and avoid seeing Justin and Dylan. I bump into Lo. Oh no! She follows me on to the bus.

'Emily, your mum came into the surgery! She went crazy at Rod. She says she'll dump him if he doesn't cut up your cousin John's gums! Except I'm sure that Rod still thinks Neville Barton is your cousin John . . .'

I groan and tune out.

Lo's still raving on when the bus stops at the billboard of Yarradindi Doug and Marilyn Monroe, where, speak of the devil, is Neville Barton himself. He's dressed in his trademark, chest-high shorts, telling off some handicapped man about parking. Suddenly, out of the corner of my eye, I glimpse *another Neville!* He's lurking in the background watching the real one. They're dressed identically, but while the real Neville's scrawny and freckled, the other one's tall and burly with legs and arms covered in curly black fur . . .

Wait a minute!
Rod?

The bus jolts off. I desperately scan the crowds, but the furry Neville has disappeared. I turn to Lo.

'Lo, that wasn't ... that couldn't be ...'

'Rod? Yes, I told you. He thinks Neville is John. And you see, everyone keeps saying John looks sexy!'

I jump off the bus at the traffic lights and walk to the wharf. My head is spinning. The world has gone mad. Rod dressing like Neville so Blanche will think he's sexy! I'm surrounded by love-sick maniacs.

I *am* a love-sick maniac.

And it's got to stop. I can't go on hopelessly loving someone who doesn't even realise I exist.

And then I see him. *John* ...

He's brought the launch to meet me! I melt! Our hands touch as he smiles and helps me aboard.

(Why isn't this happening in slow motion?)

He leans over and murmurs softly.

'Now, there's only ... Trixie ...'

'Trixie?'

I'm about to ask who Trixie is, but then I twig. Reality buckets over me like cold water. A battered Toyota Corolla has just pulled up near the wharf. A long leg extends from the driver's seat. It pulls out behind it a wheelbarrow of melons crammed into a body stocking. The body stocking waves and giggles and puts on a floppy straw hat. It capers up with melons colliding and feet flicking outwards. It makes a big fuss of crossing its legs and bouncing its dangling foot idly.

Rupert Murdoch. Where are you now that I need you?

Chapter 22

'Miss Simpson is a freak.'

I have written this on my Australian history textbook next to an illustration of Captain Cook bending out over the side of the *Endeavour* with a telescope pressed to his eye. Someone has drawn a little cloud coming out of the back of his knee breeches and the word 'fart'. I'm sitting in my room doing my homework.

John and Miss Simpson are on the verandah outside my window, translating business letters. Miss Simpson is showing off like mad. John's shorts and bare chest have driven her into a frenzy. She chatters away in her fake Japanese voice. She goes off into peals of girlish laughter. Tiff brings them coffee and biscuits. Miss Simpson thanks her in Japanese. She then explains to

Tiff what she has just said and what Tiff should reply. John makes admiring noises. Tiff replies in an even more fake voice.

Vomit.

I try to concentrate on my homework, but my mind keeps wandering. I have to finish soon because Tiff is giving a farewell party for Martin. Martin and his family are moving to the mainland. Now that John has arranged for the kelp to be transported by a truck company, our truck's not needed, so Martin's out of a job. He's going to some garage up north. Tiff is making savouries. Very wisely, John has arranged for Aunt Ruby to pick up some KFC from the mainland on her last ferry run.

I force myself through the history homework, ignoring the giggles and Japanese flutings from outside the window. Only maths to go. But my eye falls on the plans for the new plant that John gave me. John's had an architect do some rough sketches of our new plant. It looks wonderful. It's all concrete and it's got its own jetty. All the bits are labelled in the architect's beautiful italic handwriting. I idly flick my plate off and on.

'Processing Area ... Drying Area ... North Beach ...'

North Beach? The plant is to be built on North Beach!

I gag because I've nearly swallowed my plate with surprise. How can John dream of putting the plant on North Beach! I run out to the balcony. No-one's there. I run down to the beach. Miss Simpson is nowhere to be seen, but John is sitting on the sand up from the jetty. I run up, still clutching the plans.

'John! John!'

'What's the matter?'

'These plans! The plant's on the North Beach!'

John's casual.

'Oh yes, that was the architect's idea. It's not happening.'

He leans over and points at the plans.

'He wanted it there because there's no kelp on North Beach. On *this* beach, the kelp is so thick that we might have problems with jammed propellers on boats coming in to transport the stuff out. But unless we build a really huge plant, double the size of this one, it's not worth the expense.'

I breathe a sigh of relief. I smile. Things are looking up. Miss Simpson's gone home and I have him to myself.

'So,' I grin. 'You've sent old Trixie home?'

'Oh she hasn't gone,' says John. 'She's getting changed for a swim.'

He nods his head towards the house. And at that moment, far worse than my nightmare of her and John, Miss Simpson appears. She is in a bikini.

John gets up.

'There she is now. Joining us for a dip?'

I feel a surge of fury. How could he! Couldn't he do better than that! Miss Simpson ... ! Trixie! Sounds like a rotten poodle! Miss Simpson does her ballerina's run along the sand. It's grotesque. The fabric of the bikini is strained to breaking point. Every bulge is fighting for its freedom. I think of Nanny Ethel's advice, 'Never trust a Tate.'

I sniff.

'No way I'm going swimming here. Not with all the kelp.'

But I stay and watch. Through narrowed eyes. I'm eaten up with jealousy but I can't leave. John soon gives up fighting the kelp. He comes and sits with me. I'm not forgiving him.

Miss Simpson plunges off the jetty. She

plunges off the boats. She ploughs up and down doing backstroke. She ploughs up and down doing freestyle. She ploughs up and down doing butterfly, windmilling her arms madly and breathing with an athlete's precision. She bobs up and down in the water, doing her 'little peal of bells' laugh. I yawn pointedly. Her big mistake is to try to stand on her hands in the water. It shows off her legs brilliantly. But when she surfaces she's tangled up in an enormous clump of Bobbly Brains. I give a big snorty laugh. Even John cracks up. But then—I can't believe it—he goes and untangles her. She makes it last.

Martin's farewell party is a bit sad. John keeps urging him to stay. He wants Martin to drive the new tractor and trailer we're getting to transport the kelp along the beaches to the plant. But Martin's mind's made up. He goes and pats the old truck. We all get sentimental. Martin runs his hand across the leather driver's seat. An owl nesting on the clutch nips his thumb. Tiff has to get him a bandaid.

Blanche arrives home late from the Supa Market and John gives her a note reading, 'Sandwich?' She scrawls beneath it, 'Not even if I was starving!'

Next morning the new tractor arrives at 6.00 am. It's actually second hand, but it's gleaming like new. I stroll dozily out into the sunlight to join the crowd. John, who has driven a tractor heaps of times in his vineyard in France, is going to explain how to drive it. I'm just in time to hear John tell Clem that he will be the one to drive the tractor and trailer.

Clem beams with pride then breaks out in a cold sweat. John hops up onto the tractor and explains the controls. It has heaps of dials and two gear sticks. I get on the ferry and as it pulls away I see John explaining the uses of the different sticks. Clem is constantly nodding his head. He shifts from foot to foot. I realise he is in a total panic. Col, standing nearby, is refusing to watch.

As we reach the mainland, a cheerful-looking middle-aged woman carrying a suitcase approaches the gangplank. She asks me if this is the ferry to Tate Island. Aunt Ruby whispers that it's Mrs Lee, our new housekeeper. What's more, she's a fantastic cook. Oh John, is there no end to your brilliance . . . !

Chapter 23

On the school bus, Justin blocks my way. His eyes are full of pain and his mouth tugs down at the corners.

I don't know what to do. Then I think of the soapies and I say, 'Justin, I need some space.' I stumble up the bus to sit next to Jennifer Bates. But the place is occupied.

By Vince.

Jennifer's all fluttery. She's blinking a lot. Vince smiles his Monopoly smile.

Big deal, Vince, I think to myself.

But I'm cut. I slide into a vacant double seat and close my eyes. I feel someone sit beside me. This whole thing is ridiculous. Why is Justin interested in me? What do I have to do to get rid of him? Why doesn't he just go away? Suddenly, my nostril gets flicked, hard. I hear a high-pitched giggle. I don't need to open my eyes to know who's responsible.

Dylan flicks my nostril again. I ignore him. He flicks it again. I open my eyes, bellow and thump him on the arm. Justin comes bounding up the bus and socks Dylan. Dylan's laughing happily. He's a psychopath. The bus pulls over in front of Woolworth's. Yarradindi Doug beams beerily at the world. He is preferring his beer to a champion race horse.

I'm hiding in the computer room when Sophie walks in followed by Justin. Sophie says, 'Justin wants to know what you got against him.'

'I haven't got anything against him. I just ...' (thank heaven for the soapies), '... I'm just not ready to make a commitment.'

Justin doesn't say anything.

Sophie says, 'Justin says, does that mean you're not in Lies for the concert?'

Think fast. Justin might look pathetic, but he is the boy who once punched a hole through the Biology Lab door because he was angry.

'Well,' I reply, 'it's up to you. If you want me to stay, I'll stay.'

Sophie says, 'Justin says he wants you to stay.'

Justin must be communicating by telepathy because he hasn't said a word. Does he need Sophie to talk because he can't? Or is it because he's chief of the gang, and therefore it's beneath him to do his own talking? The only sure thing is that Sophie is glaring at me with total contempt. Justin stirs expectantly. What to do?

I cough. I polish my glasses. I say, 'Okay.'

Which is how I come to kiss Justin.

I stress that while I did not want to kiss Justin, Justin did not force me. I had to make a split-second decision. Since I've never been properly kissed, I decided that, all things considered, I needed the practice.

It happens at lunchtime. It's rehearsal time for the school concert number and Lies is assembling. I've been given a tambourine to play. I play exactly the same sort of thing that I did in kindergarten, except now my tambourine has no ribbons or drum bit in the middle. Also, I have to glower at the audience, rather than wave to my relatives and remember to go to the toilet beforehand. Justin wants us to spit at the audience. Mr Thompson agrees that this is an artistic statement, but reckons the spit might accidentally fall into the equipment and cause a short circuit. We settle for shouted insults.

We've stopped because the keyboard player is having trouble with his speakers. I go outside to eat my cheese sandwich. Just as I'm removing my plate, I catch a powerful whiff of Brut. Justin's staring at me dolefully. I look away and put my plate inside my lunch box. It somehow reminds me of a cute and cheerful little animal. A little crab, maybe.

Justin is building up to say something. A great wave of boredom flows over me. If he were Vince, we could crack jokes. If he were John, I could swoon and admire his five o'clock shadow. As it is, I realise I'm more interested in a conversation with my plate than with the person Year Nine reckons is my boyfriend.

'What's up, man?' he says sadly.

I shrug. I don't mind him calling me

'man'. The Cools call everyone 'man', even the ladies in the canteen. It's a gesture of friendship. They call him 'darl'.

There's a pause. He leans miserably against the wall. He says croakily, 'Last night . . .'

He's really choked. His voice is so low I can hardly hear him.

'. . . Me dad . . . me dad give me the money for a whole KFC mega meal and . . .'

There's a long pause. He plays with his skull key ring. He takes some short breaths then blurts out tragically, 'I couldn't eat it!'

Give me a break!

I hate myself. How can I be so heartless? A KFC mega meal is a high point on Justin's calendar and he's nearly in tears.

'Look, Justin . . .'

'Are you dumping me?'

How can I dump you? We were never together. Or did I doze off and miss something? I have a flash of panic. Maybe I did. Maybe I was daydreaming about John and I agreed to go steady with Justin. Maybe to marry Justin. Maybe I am already married to Justin and I've been asleep for five years.

'Tell me, man! I gotta know!'

He sits down beside me.

'D'you love me?'

Oh no! He's desperate. I've never seen his eyes so wide open. I don't know what to say. I'm drowning.

'Justin, I . . . I really like you.' (*Actually, I don't really like you. Actually, I wouldn't really care if I never saw you again. In fact if you dropped off the planet tomorrow it wouldn't worry me much, and besides, I think your armpits are giving me hayfever.*)

It's at this point I begin to think about how horrible I am. How I would feel if John thought this about me? Perhaps he does think this about me? After all, at breakfast yesterday he hardly spoke to me, and . . .

I suddenly catch sight of Justin's face. He's beaming. Justin. This is the first time in years I've seen his teeth. First his eyes, now his teeth. I panic. What did he say? What did I say?

'Justin . . .?'

'You really like me?'

'Yes, but . . .'

Just as I'm trying to think how I can tell him I don't want to see him again, he puts his face close up to mine. He's also using mouthwash.

He croaks, 'Kiss me, man.'

I panic and do some very quick thinking. First thought: yuk! Second thought: I need to know if my plate will get caught up in John's mouth because there are a lot of dumb jokes about this sort of thing. Third thought: I need to know how to position my nose. Fourth thought: I need to know if kissing will dislodge my glasses.

I snap my plate back in and kiss Justin. I barely notice the kiss, which is a sort of nothing, clammy-cherry sensation. It's like kissing Cinnamon without the biscuity smell. But (good news) my plate doesn't engage, and (bad news) our noses brush. I kiss him again to get the nose right. Still wrong. I tilt my head the other way. Better, but the glasses tip.

I seize Justin's cheeks in my hands because it's really important that I kiss John perfectly. I aim this time. I'm just scanning his face to check I've got the angles right when I see he's looking at me in pleased amazement. He seems to have stopped breathing.

I realise that from his point of view I have been kissing him passionately.

I pull away in horror.

Chapter 24

Idiot! Idiot! Idiot! Idiot!

I briskly say, 'Right then, lunch,' and stuff my cheese sandwich in my mouth.

I know that I am using Justin and he certainly doesn't seem to mind. But it is no excuse! The bigger problem is how I'm ever going to get rid of him ...

Playing for time, I gulp down my chocolate milk. Without pausing for breath, I stuff my banana. All the time, Justin is watching me with enormous, adoring eyes. I s'pose he thinks all that passion has given me an appetite. I'm really feeling guilty. And how can I say I don't like him when I've practically worn his lips to the bone?

When it's time for rehearsal, Justin tries to take my hand, but when I don't accept, he doesn't seem to mind. He shuffles alongside me loyally. In the middle of 'Lover', I do my two shakes and a wrist-bash on the tambourine. I catch him smiling at me. He's catatonic with infatuation. I realise Justin has never been kissed either. Or rather, he's never been kissed quite like that. How am I going to get out of this mess? A month ago I was the class dag. Now I am the wildest kisser in Year Nine. The only positive thing is that Dylan has been given a three-day suspension.

As I come out of school, Lo pounces.

'Em, your mum made me give her John Tate's address! I mean, Neville's address!'

'You don't mean she's planning to go to his house!'

'She's already been, and, oh Em ...'

Lo's pale.

'What—did she find out about the mix-up?'

'I don't know! All I know is what I overheard her telling Rod. Em, she thinks Neville and his wife must be helping John to sabotage the island! She's out to get Neville as well!'

I groan.

On the ferry home I close my eyes. I close my eyes a lot these days, partly because it helps me to concentrate on John, but mostly because it shuts out the series of disasters that is my life at the moment. As we draw towards the island wharf, I open them. To see Clem and Col outside the factory shouting at each other.

I have only seen this once before. This was when they fell out over a competition to win a year's supply of dog food. Col didn't want to enter because they didn't have a dog. Clem argued that when they won the year's supply of food they could afford a dog. And anyhow, he wanted a dog whether they won or not. A dog is the only thing that causes problems between Col and Clem. It rarely comes up because we aren't allowed dogs on the island—it's a wildlife reserve. But the dog is still a dream of Clem's. Every year I buy him a dog calendar for Christmas. He plans to call the dog 'Prince'.

But today they aren't arguing about Prince. They're arguing about the tractor. Clem's on it, Col's next to it and John is trying to get a word in edgeways. Which is difficult because he has Tiff's twins swarming all over him.

I take John aside.

'What's been happening?'

John looks drawn.

'Clem's driving so slowly! He's spent all day moving two loads! I'm going to have to get another driver. Take these kids, will you . . .'

I'm sad for Clem. I take Tiff's twins by the hand and set off towards the house. Who will John get to drive the tractor? One of the aunties? Surely not. One of the mainland Tates? It never occurs to me that he will ask Col. As I get to the house, I say hello to the cheery Mrs Lee, our new housekeeper. She's scrubbing clean a mountain of assorted rubber boots and singing 'Jumping Jack Flash'. I glance over my shoulder. I'm appalled. Because I can see that Clem is off the tractor and Col is getting on. I go racing down the beach.

'John! No!'

The problem is that Col has never learnt to drive. The reason why Col never learnt to drive is that he can't tell left from right.

'Step on it, Col!'

Col is looking at the gleaming bank of controls on the dashboard. For one blissful second I think I will be in time.

Then Col steps on it.

If Clem has always wanted a dog, so Col has dreamt of speed. He beams gratitude at John. He swivels the gear sticks about. He slams down his foot and roars off. Backwards.

We all scream. Col clings panic-stricken to the steering wheel.

John shouts, 'Change your selection! Get a low gear!'

Col wrenches the gear sticks furiously. 'No, left! left!'

Col pulls the stick on the right. Then he tries the stick on the left. Then the right. The machine hiccups, roars, the trailer jerks along bouncing. The kelp flies off. The only thing the tractor doesn't do is stop. It's roaring backwards towards the drying shed.

John runs frantically towards it. He's within seconds of reaching it when Col miraculously gets out of reverse. He stops. John beams. Col wrenches the gears—and accelerates forward. Straight at him. John does the neatest backwards run I've seen. It's like an Irish dance. He's yelling: 'The brake! Left foot!'

Col slams down his right foot. Then his left foot. Then his right foot. He wrenches madly at the gear sticks.

'No! Left! Left!'

It's no good. Now Col's bouncing and

careering at top speed towards the seal fence. He's hanging onto the little wheel for dear life. He yells in panic.

John shouts, 'Jump off! Jump off, Col!'

But Col grips the wheel as if he's glued to it. He hits the fence. He ploughs on through, dragging about ten metres of fence with him, posts and all. The seals charge ahead of the sweeping fence, barking madly. Albatrosses fly up, squawking.

John pounds up to me. He is breathless, at a loss for words. We stare at Col, who is rapidly disappearing up the beach at the rear of an army of demented galloping blobs. His yells hang in the wind.

The world's only seal drover.

John shakes his head.

'It's got to run out of petrol sooner or later.'

Col does two and a half circuits of the island before the petrol runs out. He pretends it was all deliberate and he was just going for a drive. John gently explains to Col and Clem that he will be getting a driver from the mainland.

Col and Clem are not talking.

The evening is saved by our new housekeeper Mrs Lee, who cooks like an angel.

She also bursts into snatches of song as she's serving and tells bad knock-knock jokes, but nobody's complaining. She does Beatles hits with the soup (tomato—home-made). She does Michael Jackson with the main course (roast lamb with mint sauce and cauliflower) and Whitney Houston with the dessert (apple crumble with custard).

The kitchen is gleaming and about five metres of junk have been cleared from the hall.

It's not until I'm in bed that I realise Blanche has not come home tonight at all.

Chapter 25

I'm standing on the island jetty and I'm really angry with John. Dylan Pocky is fishing and Cinnamon is chalking a picture on the boards. John comes up and asks me what is the matter. I turn away. He says, 'No, Em, you have to look at me.' I turn and look at him. He's wearing his blue open-necked shirt. He takes me by the arms. He's staring at me. I suddenly realise. He's going to kiss me! I hold my breath. I stare into his green eyes ...

Something is shaking me violently. Something soft and feathery is pressing up to my face. I wake up, half-smothered. Without my glasses everything is blurred. Five centimetres away from my left eyeball there is ... another eyeball! It's massive, round and vacant! It bulges out of a gigantic, brown face. A feathery face! With a beak!

I scream and leap in the air. There's a giant chicken in bed with me! Aunt Ruby is standing by my bed trying to hush me. I realise that John was a dream. The reality is Aunt Ruby trying to shove her pet chook, Feathers, under my pillow.

'Em! Quick! She's after Feathers!'

'What?'

My heart is pounding with shock. Feathers is crooning quietly. She's jerking her head around and staring vacantly out of her round glassy eyes. She gives off a warm musty smell.

'Mrs Lee!' hisses Ruby. 'She's cleaning the house from top to bottom. She says Feathers has to live in the chook pen. She can't, Em! She's used to blankets!'

I groan. The best dream I've ever had has been interrupted by a refugee chook. I close my eyes and plunge into darkness after John. John! Come back! Where were we?

'No, Em, wake up! I've got to take in the 6.30 am ferry!'

The wharf. Got it. Dylan Pocky and Cinnamon. Got them. Now John. He's returning ... I'm even managing to block out Aunt Ruby, who's rabbiting on about

Mrs Lee cleaning the house with bleach. John says: 'No, Em, you have to look at me . . .'

Ow! Ouch! What was that!

It's a chook claw gouging my arm. Feathers is now walking stiffly up and down on top of me, jerking her head about and scratching with her claws. I think she's establishing her territory.

'Oh look, she likes you!'

Feathers pecks experimentally at the covers.

'Auntie Ruby, *please* go away . . .' I whine pathetically.

There's a rapid knocking at my door. Ruby freezes.

'Emily?'

It's Mrs Lee.

'Yes?'

'Knock, knock . . .'

'What?'

'Knock, knock.'

I wilt. It's 6.00 am, a chook is trying to nest on my stomach and the house-keeper wants to play 'knock-knock' jokes.

'Who's there?' I respond half-heartedly.

'Ahmed.'

'Ahmed who?'

'Ahmed you bacon and eggs.'

She goes into a peal of laughter. We hear her footsteps fading up the hall. Aunt Ruby's looking at me piteously.

'Please, Emily. Yours is the tidiest room. She'd never think to look here.'

Feathers cocks her head and looks at me. Auntie Ruby cocks her head and looks at me.

We put Feathers in my wardrobe. She walks up and down over my shoes. She pecks at the lace holes. She grabs the lace from one of my old running shoes and tugs at it.

Auntie Ruby croons, 'Love her, she's pretending it's a worm.'

Feathers isn't pretending. She's trying to swallow it. I close the wardrobe door. I put on my glasses. I hope I don't come home to find her dead. Actually, at this moment I couldn't care less. I couldn't care if I came home and found two dead pterodactyls in my wardrobe. I'm trying to cling on to my dream . . .

It's no good. Gone . . .

At breakfast John is wearing his blue shirt.

Mrs Lee makes us scrambled eggs, sausages, bacon, tomatoes, toast and orange juice.

Halfway through, the door bursts open and Blanche enters, wild-eyed, from the ferry. She looks exhausted. She has twigs in her hair and the heel of one shoe is missing. Has she been stalking Neville? Has she been camping out in his garden? As we all stare in amazement, Blanche gathers herself up, and, with enormous dignity, limps past, clumping on her broken shoe. The door closes behind her. Nobody says a word.

I stagger to the ferry with my stomach bulging. As I get on the bus, Justin is wearing a heavy metal T-shirt and a smile that practically splits his face in half. I sit down on the bus and close my eyes. Throughout History I close my eyes. But my brain is working overtime. Lunchtime creeps nearer. How can I avoid Justin? Spend my whole school career with my eyes closed? I rack my brains. Go to the sick room? Justin could follow. Sit in the girls' toilets? Justin could talk to me through the back windows. Time's running out. Then I think of it. I'll hang around with Lo!

Of course, Lo is away from school that day. Thanks, Lo. You even cause problems by not being there.

Finally, I figure if I stick with teachers, not even Justin will have the nerve to go into a clinch. As soon as the lunch bell rings, I hurry to the staff room. I will waylay a teacher. I will keep one in conversation about problems with my work.

I haven't bargained on how much the teachers value their time away from us. It's like a cattle stampede. I practically get trampled. I stop Mr Williams, my History teacher and tell him I don't understand the reasons for distress and discontent in the fledgling colony. He says, 'Read the book', and crunches over my feet with his Docs. I'm desperate. Justin looms.

Then, reprieve. I see old Mrs Hurley toiling up the corridor with her Bible stories book and her family-sized box of Maltesers.

'Mrs Hurley, I need to talk to you.'

'Certainly dear, come to the staff room in half an hour.'

'No, no, it's urgent! I need to talk to you now!'

Mrs Hurley sighs. She looks done in.

'Well, if it's really important. What is

181

it, dear? Problems with homework?'

'No, no, I . . .'

'Something at home? Perhaps I could book you in with the school counsellor.'

I see Justin giving himself a squirt of breath freshener.

'No, no, I need to talk to you. Now. It must be now!'

What excuse can I make? Why would it be vital for me to talk to the Catholic Religious Instruction teacher?

'I . . . I . . .'

I gulp. She's staring at me. Justin snaps on the cap of his breath freshener. I have a flash of inspiration.

'I want to become a nun.'

I spend the whole lunchtime inventing a religious experience. Since I'm no good at English, I base it on an episode of the *X Files* where aliens with flies' heads use their virus-packed saliva to take over the world. Mrs Hurley gets very worried. When I describe the special effects, she drops her box of Maltesers and suggests an appointment with the school counsellor. We agree to continue our talk after school.

After school I run for the public bus. I look out of the bus window and see Mrs Hurley, the counsellor, the school principal and an elderly clergyman all looking anxiously around the asphalt.

As I get off the ferry I meet Tiff and the children getting on. They're going in for a dental check-up with Rod. Tiff's all giggly about Rod. I open my mouth to say her love is hopeless, then shut it. Like me, she needs her dreams.

I walk past the tractor. It is being driven by a fat man with a beer belly. I feel a twinge for Col and Clem, but John's absolutely right to get another driver.

Ms Emily Tate
Tate Island
Victoria
Australia

Dear Ms Tate,

Mr Murdoch thanks you for your kind letter and wishes you every success in your chosen career.
Yours sincerely,

F W Paterson

*For and on behalf of
Rupert Murdoch*

In my room, Feathers is not dead,
although when I see how much chook poo
there is all over my shoes, I feel like killing
her myself. The smell is appalling. I spray
the room with some perfume called
'Mountain Flowers' that Col and Clem
gave me for Christmas. Great. Mountain
Flowers and chook sweat. Feathers, in the
meantime, is refusing to move from my
tennis shoe. Ruby has warned me. She
says I'm not to worry about it. It just
means that Feathers is building up to
laying an egg.

This is a load off my mind.

I lift up Feathers' closest wing and give
her a squirt of Mountain Flowers. She
blinks. I flop on my bed and start a letter
to Mr Murdoch.

*Mr Rupert Murdoch
News Limited
United States of America*

Dear Mr Murdoch,

Following the exciting renovations to our kelp processing plant, I am planning on leaving school as soon as possible . . .

Outside my window I hear a familiar giggle and some fluting Japanese. John and 'The Legs' have arrived back for more translations. I feel a surge of irritation. I'm wasting my time on John. How can I fall for a man who sells himself so cheaply? Although I must admit, he hasn't ever shown any signs of being attracted to Miss Simpson. (Not that he's shown any signs of being attracted to me.)

'Knock knock!'

This woman has a serious problem.

It turns out that Mrs Lee has baked a whole pile of shortbread biscuits and wants to know if I'd like some. I sigh. At least it will get me away from old Trixie.

I sit in the gleaming kitchen. I grimly pack away about twenty shortbread fingers as Mrs Lee sings hits from *Grease* and scrubs the ceiling. Then she scrubs the walls, the inside of the cupboards, the outside of the cupboards and all the paintwork. She also throws salt in the air and tapes brown paper over all the windows. She leans over to me and whispers confidentially, 'It baffles their radar.'

I eat three more shortbread biscuits.

Blanche is still at work when the Principal rings, so Mrs Lee takes the call. The Principal says that the school is worried because I have told Mrs Hurley there are fly-headed aliens on Tate Island. Mrs Lee tuts irritably. She says I have far too vivid an imagination. She says that the aliens on Tate Island are much more like crabs and use simple laser guns.

My feeling is, so what? If she can cook like this, I don't care if she's an alien herself.

Nobody else seems to have noticed that Mrs Lee is completely deranged. John is working late in the office and doesn't want to be disturbed. Tiff is occupied making clothes for the children. Auntie Ruby is sitting in my wardrobe ready to chuck a cloth over Feathers' head if she clucks. She has my radio going quietly because Feathers likes golden oldies.

Blanche comes home, gets an urgent phone call from Rod and leaves again for the mainland in Grandpa's boat. I don't even want to imagine what she's doing.

I walk along the beach. The factory is working nights, now, with different shifts of workers from the mainland. The plant shines white, glinting under rows of new spotlights. Fatty whimpers from behind the seal fence (which John had fixed this morning). I walk down to the caravan park. I go to visit Clem and Col. Clem is sitting outside cutting out coupons from a cereal pack. I can see Col's shadow inside the van. I can see he's listening to everything we say.

'What's the competition, Clem?'

He grunts. I can see his heart's not in it.

'Shop till you drop.'

'What do you win?'

'Oh, I don't know, Em. I think you get a free trip to Sydney and as much as you can spend on clothes in three hours.'

I've never seen Clem in any other clothes apart from his best suit and his work clothes. Maybe there are dozens of different rubber boots on sale in the city.

'Why do you want to win that?'

Clem stirs and snips for a moment. He pushes his glasses back up his nose.

'I don't want *him* to win . . .'

He jerks his head towards the van. Inside, Col gets up and walks away. I don't know what to say. I've never known a fight to go on between them for so long. I offer to help with a slogan, but Clem is prickly. He says he's making up his own slogans now. I sense that this is in response to something that Col has taunted him about. Clem's slogan is: 'I want to shop till I drop because . . . I want to.'

Back along the beach, a row of seagulls is sitting on the seal fence facing the wind. I wonder which is Grandpa. Perhaps they're all Tates. I wonder what they think of the island now that hardly any Tates are working on it. I suddenly remember the old days—with all the aunties and uncles kidding and laughing on the beach. I find myself smiling. I miss it . . .

Miss it! I have to be joking! The bickering, the inefficiency, the mess! Not to mention no John!

No John!

At 11.00 pm we get a call from the police station. They tell us that Blanche and Rod have been arrested after an incident outside the bowling club.

Chapter 26

Dylan Pocky's dad had caught Rod creeping around the back. I suppose he'd been tailing Neville. The policeman says Terry Pocky karate-chopped Rod. Then Blanche appeared on the scene and went for Terry, who tried to grab her. Brave man. Apparently, one of Blanche's long dangly earrings got caught in Terry Pocky's hair. When the police arrived they were locked together like two fighting scorpions.

John and I go to bail out Blanche. As we walk in we see Blanche and Rod. Rod has a black eye and is still dressed like Neville. Blanche is demanding her rights and threatening to sue everyone.

When she sees us, she says, 'About time.' She turns back to the policeman and says, 'This is my cousin, John Tate. He will tell you I am a gardening expert and I was in the carpark of the bowling club purely to inspect the landscaping.'

Rod exclaims, 'This isn't John Tate!'

'Of course it is!' hisses Blanche. 'Who do *you* think it is?'

Rod literally staggers.

He gasps, 'But the man we've been following . . .?'

Blanche snorts. 'That's Neville!'

'*Neville*? Who the hell's Neville? You said "Follow the old man"! John Tate's the old man.'

They have a blazing row, which Blanche brings to a close by telling Rod he's dumped.

The police let them off with a warning. As we leave, Blanche stalks ahead of us. I look back at Rod. His shoulders are drooped. He's staring hopelessly after Blanche. I know how he feels.

We get home at about midnight. Auntie Ruby is sleeping on my floor to be near Feathers in her moment of egg-laying triumph. I squirt some more Mountain Flowers into the air and turn out the light.

The phone is ringing. And ringing. And

ringing. I tut to myself and stumble out to answer it. It's 3.30 am.

A deep voice is gabbling gibberish. This is Dylan's idea of a joke.

I say, 'Get lost, Dylan, you pinhead.'

A woman's voice responds, ''Allo? Is thees Tet Eye-lend?'

Kylie? Sophie?

Suddenly, my whole stomach turns over. I know who it is.

'I would laik to spik to Jon-Pol. I am Babette. Hees waif.'

I'm suddenly wide-awake. I stand there motionless as the last month flashes past me.

'I'll just get him.'

I hammer on John's door, which used to be Grandpa's door. I go in, calling 'John?'

I can see him in the darkness. He's propping himself on his elbow.

He croaks, 'Em? What is it?'

'Your wife's on the phone.'

The effect is amazing. He sits bolt upright, then jumps out of bed, grabbing his dressing gown. I'm wishing I was in my new satiny dressing gown instead of my old towelling one, but John doesn't even look at me. He's frowning. His mouth is pulled down like Justin's on the bus.

He picks up the phone and starts talking anxiously in French. I hear Fifi, or whatever her name is, laughing and gabbling at the other end. John listens. He suddenly beams. He says something which makes her laugh.

My heart sinks. I drag myself slowly to the kitchen as John's French voice gargles on happily behind me. I hate the French voice. I don't know him with that voice. I remove the brown paper Mrs Lee has sellotaped all over the electric jug. I start to make tea.

I knew this would happen. And she doesn't even want him.

John enters. The smile on his face cuts me like a knife.

'Ah! You're making tea! Good idea!'

Stop smiling, you idiot!

He doesn't. He strides around beaming.

I say, casually, 'How is she?'

'Fine. Working hard.'

His face must be about to split. I'm furious. I hate this woman but I need to know more. I spoon in the tea-leaves.

'What does she do?'

'Mmm?'

'What's her job?'

'She's a model.'

I stop in my tracks. Right. Good. Terrific. Miss Simpson's legs with a fabulous body on top ... At least she'll be dumb.

'That's when she's not studying medicine.'

There *are* people in the world like this. People with fantastic bodies and brilliant minds who also have amazing sporting skills and always get voted class captain. Cordelia Mortimer in my class is one. Cordelia's blazer's so weighted down with badges and labels and significant piping that any normal person would be hard-pressed just to move. But since Cordelia is state champion in the hundred metres sprint, she springs along like a deer (helped probably by her gold medal in ballet). If she did find it difficult, she could make a speech about it in three different languages. While tossing back her perfect, golden hair.

I suppose Babette is what the Cordelias become when they leave school.

I have an image of Babette going up to collect her Nobel Prize. She's doing that cat-walk stride, with her hips leading. Her shoulders are going like pistons.

'And now Babette, wearing Dior's latest summer creation, goes up to collect her Nobel Prize for astrophysics . . .'

She takes it. She strides across the stage, poses to the left, to the right, tips her head. She pivots on one perfect foot, shows the lining of her jacket and strides off to thunderous applause.

'As soon as Babette completes this year's training for France's Olympic pentathlon team, she will be developing her cure for cancer and repainting the Sistine Chapel . . .'

'Is she coming here?'

'Here? Good Lord, no. She's much too busy.'

Oh well, of course, who'd come here!

I say, poisonously, 'I guess she'd find it pretty boring.'

He chuckles. 'To tell the truth, she finds *me* pretty boring. All the business and stuff.'

I can't believe it! This woman is insane! John, boring!

And yet he's smiling! He's happy just to have talked to her! I'm seething. I want to let him know that he means nothing to me. I start gabbling on about how much

I, too, hate the island and want to leave. This is intended to make him persuade me to stay. But he doesn't. So I go further. I say how I'm dying to leave school. How I'd kill to go to the school for girls with potential for commerce.

He nods sympathetically and drinks his tea. Not once does he say he'll miss me. Not once.

I go to my room as the sun is rising. I open my drawer and get out the macadamia nut bag in which John's fingers touched mine. Tears come to my eyes. I let them roll down my cheeks. I taste one.

Oh John. Over you I break my heart.

Chapter 27

I wake up to the most hysterical squawking from Feathers. Ruby is trying to shut her up.

'What's wrong with her?'

'She's laid an egg!'

'She sounds as if she's dying!'

'Oh no, she's always like this! It's triumph!'

It sounds like sheer terror to me. Feathers' normally blank eyes are panic-stricken. I wonder if she remembers she lays eggs. Maybe it comes as a surprise each time. And what a surprise! No wonder she's going berserk.

I help Ruby out of the back door clutching Feathers and the egg. It's now 5.30 am.

I go to the kitchen. John's cup is still there and someone is hiding in the pantry.

It's Tiff with a twin under each arm.

She sighs with relief and says, 'Thank heavens it's you, Emily. I thought it was Mrs Lee.'

'What are you doing in the pantry?'

'I was looking for the instant porridge, but everything seems to be wrapped in brown paper.'

Tiff pauses, then whimpers, 'Emily, I miss my cooking!'

It would be cruel to say she's the only one who does, so I do sympathetic murmurs.

'I *know* it wasn't as fancy as Mrs Lee's. I know it wasn't perhaps as *nicely presented* . . .'

'You're right. Mrs Lee's cooking just isn't quite the same.'

Tiff glows and she puts her arm around me.

'Emily. Let me make you a bowl of porridge.'

It takes real skill to mess up instant porridge. Tiff makes me an especially large helping for old time's sake. She hasn't put enough water in it, so it has a powdery, chalky edge to it. I say it's marvellous and wash it down with gallons of tea.

I set off on the early ferry. Auntie Ruby is at the helm. She waves. Feathers is sitting next to her. I plan today's speech to Mrs Hurley about getting 'the calling'. This should take up all of lunch hour again and save me from Justin.

As we sail away from the island I start to get a stomach ache. It must be the tea swelling the porridge. As we come into the mainland wharf, I'm in real pain. My stomach starts to make strange noises. It squeaks and growls. I get a bit alarmed.

I pat it experimentally with my hands. It's tight as a drum. How much more can this porridge swell? I feel liquid swirling. Inside me, bubbles rise and pop. Is it cooking in there?

This is all I need.

I stagger onto the public bus. A lively conversation is going on between my gastric juices. I'm in agony but I have to stand. I'm right next to a boy from Year Eleven when the noise starts getting louder and louder. It's astonishing. It gets louder and louder. It's alive. Everyone looks round. I want to die. It stops.

I breathe again. I chicken-wing and look casual. The bus swoops past the new Ocean Meadows housing development and stops at the lights. Everything's quiet. I think of John and Babette. I bet she's beautiful. I get a lump in my throat . . .

Suddenly, a knife turns in my stomach and it starts the loudest, longest creak. Then it squeals. Then it creaks again and squirts. It's moving about of its own accord. I feel as if my skin is going to split. It's like a horror movie. Any minute now a giant spear of asparagus is going to explode out of my navel. The boy from Year Eleven starts smirking. My face burns. Why do these things happen to me?

At the next stop I leap off. I limp to school. It must be the combination of Mrs Lee's cooking and Tiff's. My system can't take such extremes.

Mrs Hurley meets me at the gate. My heart sinks. There goes lunchtime. She has brought a Catholic youth worker to meet me. He's about forty and wears a basketball cap back-to-front as a sign of coolness.

We sit in a little room next to the staff room. My stomach moans and gurgles to itself, but it's calming down. He pretends not to notice.

He's seen the episode of the *X Files*

with the fly people. We agree that my religious experience was probably caused by the stress of being a month behind in my English homework. He says I won't have to do it.

He gives me brochures on stress and diet and a sex education one called: 'Now You Are Growing Up'. As usual with these things, it has a man and a woman standing side by side. They are both smiling placidly even though they have no clothes on and someone has taken out the entire contents of their lower bodies apart from their gonads.

'Hey honey, I thought all we had to remove was our clothes.'

That's Vince's joke from last year's sex education classes. I really miss Vince. I wonder if he tells Jennifer jokes like these. Jennifer! And now Babette. Tate men really do pick them. I think of Nanny Ethel's advice: 'Never trust a Tate'.

Now I have to think of something to do at lunch to avoid Justin. Oh blow Justin ... I've got more important things on my mind. What if John wants to go back to his wife? What if he walks out on me?

'Eh, Tate!'

It's Sophie, with her most vicious look.

Justin's behind her. And behind Justin is Kylie Wallop.

Sophie shouts, 'Justin says, what's your problem?'

I look at her. She really annoys me. My stomach is still strangling itself.

'Eh, dur-brain!' she continues. 'Justin says what's your problem?'

'Justin says nothing. Justin's standing there like a constipated trout. So *you* tell *him* if he wants to talk to me, open his mouth.'

He does open his mouth. Actually, his jaw drops. So does Sophie's. So does Kylie's. So does mine! Because that wasn't my voice. That was Blanche.

I am turning into Blanche!

I really *am* turning into Blanche. This is terrifying. I hurry away. Then it occurs to me. Perhaps Blanche is only the way she is because of indigestion. Perhaps a lifetime of terrible cooking has made her what she is ... I never knew my Grannie, but family legend has it that Tiff took over the cooking because she was so much better at it than Gran. It doesn't bear thinking about.

I hear someone running up behind me. It's Justin.

'Eh! Em'ly!'

I turn. Justin is struggling to say something. Finally, he croaks, 'We gotta talk, man.'

'Talk about what? I'm sorry, Justin, it's over.'

'You mean ... there's someone else?'

I think of John. On the beach. At the dance. The first time I saw him. And he's in love with Babette! Tears spring into my eyes.

I shout, 'Of course there's someone else!'

My voice comes out with a catch in it. My stomach stabs.

Justin stares at me.

'Who?'

Tears blur my vision. Partly it's my stomach, but mostly it's John.

I croak, 'Isn't it obvious?'

At this moment there is a whoop. There's a wild, whirring noise. Dylan Pocky comes flying across the asphalt on his skateboard. When he's a metre away from me, he leaps off it, snatches it up and punches me on the arm. I wallop him back. He gives his high-pitched giggle. He has a new tattoo on his arm. It's a skull wrapped in snakes.

He's springing at the knees, beaming at me. Justin's face twists with jealousy.

Justin punches Dylan.

By the end of school I realise that things are a lot easier now that Justin thinks I am in love with Dylan Pocky. They just fight between themselves.

At lunchtime and recess I stay in the sewing room. I'm making my costume for our class's Drama Studies item in the concert. It's called 'The Dark Stranger of the Wolf Hour'. It's about a fourteen-year-old girl's encounter with death. I am a Spirit of the West Wind and Jennifer Bates is The Girl. Her mother is hiring her dress from a theatrical costume place. Cordelia is Beauty of the Sun. She's doing a bit of her gold-medal ballet routine at the bit where The Girl is torn between Hope and Despair.

Being Dylan's girlfriend doesn't seem to require anything of me except copping the occasional thump on the arm or a nose flick (which I return twice over). As I sit stitching my black veil, I begin to wonder whether all this bashing of the head has affected Dylan's judgement. Neither words nor physical violence will convince him that I do not love him. He just grins at me and goes, 'Dur!' I could drive an express train over him and he'd still jump up from the tracks, jam his face under my nose and go, 'Dur!'

Justin is deeply betrayed. He leans tragically against the back wall of the toilets. His cough is particularly racked. I feel a bit bad. But Sophie and Kylie stand by him like blue-haired lionesses. They make sure he has the most drags on the cigarette. Wherever he walks they march behind him like bodyguards. When they look at me in class their lips are so curled that they're practically inside out.

Now I have become Blanche, I am totally unintimidated.

It's very liberating.

At the end of sixth period I pass Miss Simpson striding leggily down the corridor. She's wearing a hot-pink smock thing over pink and black striped Lycra bike shorts. She does her witty Japanese bow. She calls me 'Emilysan' to show she's part of the family. Dream on, Baby. Actually, I feel a surge of fellow feeling. He's betrayed us both.

After school we have a run through of

our drama item. Jennifer has persuaded Vince to play the part of Social Change. He's the only boy in it. He's wearing a suit and tie with dark glasses and a hat. Halfway through he has to go off stage, then come on backwards. Just as The Girl is embracing Life (Rachel Salmon, dressed as the Sailor), Vince has to swing round and face the audience. This reveals he's now wearing a horrific Freddy Krueger mask and long fake fingernails. It's pretty effective. Ben Traversi, who's doing Lighting, shouts, 'Big improvement, Vince!' Miss Edwards tells him to shut up or leave.

Mostly, all my part involves is swaying, doing howling wind noises, and chanting: 'Death, death . . .' at the end. My big moment is right at the end of Cordelia's ballet bit. Cordelia runs on the tips of her toes across the stage. She flops with tragic elegance from the waist and you think she is going to collapse in a heap.

But then she suddenly surges upwards and stands right on the tip of one toe. She points her other leg straight out behind her and wafts her hands exquisitely above her head. This is where I come in. While Cordelia holds this position, all three Spirits of the West Wind have to get hold of her pointing leg. We walk round and round as if Cordelia is a giant screwdriver and we're screwing her foot into the stage. When we've done this three times we scatter across the stage screaming and fluttering our veils. Cordelia does a pointy-toed run off the stage, Vince shakes a fist in triumph and Jennifer dies.

Our item goes really well. But Lies is in trouble. I am no longer performing with Lies. The Cools are really angry with me and they do the logical thing. They take it out on Mr Thompson. They make rude comments about the electronic equipment he's borrowed from St Brigid's. They refuse to play 'Advance Australia Fair'. When they finally get around to playing 'Lover', there's an extra verse. It goes:

> When you betray
> The love I give
> You will be sorry, Babe,
> You ever lived.

They all look in my direction when they sing this. Now I am Blanche, I smirk and bellow, 'Ooo! Wow! I'm soooo frightened, Justin.'

Chapter 28

I get the last ferry. The island lights are on. It looks picturesque. I watch the point of light in the office of the factory. I imagine John at his desk. I wonder if he has spoken to Babette again. Babette! What kind of a name is that! Trixie and Babette. I am being rejected for a pair of performing poodles.

I make for my room. Just as I'm passing the living room, Blanche calls out to me. I go in. Now Mrs Lee's here it's incredibly tidy and looks about three times as big. Generations of Tates look down on us from the walls. You can tell what period they lived in by the style of the glasses. Blanche is resting in an armchair with her feet up. She is still in her Supa Market uniform. She is drinking tea and eating a huge piece of Mrs Lee's brilliant chocolate cake, topped with a massive blob of cream.

'Emmy, I had a call from the school today. They say you're unhappy.'

Her voice is soft. She's genuinely concerned. There really is something to the indigestion theory.

'Oh it's nothing. I made up some stuff as an excuse for not having done my English homework.'

'Are you sure?'

Blanche's huge earrings are dangling dangerously near the whipped cream and chocolate icing. It's a miracle she doesn't take her eye out when she turns round quickly.

'Well, as long as you're okay. I know things have been difficult for you since Grandpa died. They've been difficult for all of us. And John ... well, you know I don't *like* John, but who knows?'

She spoons in a large mouthful of cake and chews luxuriously.

'Perhaps he does have something to offer us.'

I'm astonished. Blanche accepting John! I know I shouldn't trust her, but this is miraculous cake. I accept a bit. Blanche hugs me and I hug her back. It's comforting, even though I get a mouthful of fluffy hair and collide with one earring.

I take John some tea, so I can look at him and yearn. I watch him work. My heart is aching. He looks tired and rumpled and the stubble on his chin is black. The little bald bit on the top of his head makes me feel oddly protective.

John, she doesn't want you ...

Maybe she does. Certainly, if she snapped her fingers, he'd come running. Maybe she has already. Maybe he's already planning to go.

He looks up, grins, and takes the tea.

'Sorry about that. Incidentally, bad news on the face pack front. The lab says the kelp is every bit as good as the most expensive mud packs from Europe. But they haven't yet found anything that can take out the green staining. They think they will find something eventually, but it'll take time. And that means money.'

'Oh, forget it.'

'Yes, well, that's what I told them. For the moment anyway.'

He sighs and rubs a hand over his eyes. He's thinking about Babette.

I need to know what's in his mind, so I ask, 'Has it been a bad day?'

'Not good. Yarradindi Beers are behaving very oddly. I have a horrible feeling something's wrong.'

That's not what you were thinking about. You were thinking about her. And you're leaving. And you don't care two hoots for me.

John looks at me.

'Em, I should tell you. If Yarradindi Beers goes bust and doesn't pay us, we'll be in big trouble.'

I'm staring at his tired face. He looks exhausted. There are dark rings around his eyes.

'Oh don't worry. They're probably not ringing because of Grandpa. He used to insult everybody. You have to talk to them through letters.'

John sighs then smiles.

'George tells me that you and Vince are in some concert tomorrow night?'

'Sort of.'

'Don't we get invited?'

I'm pleased, but I don't show it. I say casually, 'It's pretty dumb.'

'We have to come and wave the flag, though, don't we?'

'If you like.'

'Em? Is something the matter?'

I'm dying to ask him about his wife but I don't dare. Instead, I say, 'Oh no. I'm just tired.'

'Yes, Babette's phone call this morning. Sorry about that. She does tend to do things on impulse.'

Selfish too, eh?

I just have to know.

'John ... are you and Babette getting back together?'

He stares at me. His face saddens. He looks down. He picks up his pen and starts working.

Something like a little torch bulb starts to glow inside my chest.

She doesn't want him! She's ditched him! Thank you, Babette! Oh thank you!

John looks up with a forced smile and says, 'Look ... Would you excuse me? I'd like to finish this tonight.'

I leave. On wings.

Chapter 29

I sing as I brush my hair. I now have my room to myself, since Auntie Ruby and Feathers have moved into a spare van in the caravan park. Mrs Lee has scrubbed my wardrobe and shoes with disinfectant. I'm grateful I didn't have to do it. I thank her. She explains that disinfectant fouls up the aliens' sensors and stops them settling in any one place.

Mrs Lee takes Blanche her breakfast in bed. It is a huge tray loaded with scrambled eggs, bacon, tomatoes, mushrooms, coffee, toast and three sorts of jams. Mrs Lee walks down the passage singing 'I Left My Heart in San Francisco'. John isn't at breakfast. He must have been working late. Maybe he couldn't sleep because of his misery about Babette.

Ah John, never fear. I will bring you back into the ways of happiness . . .

I sing in the bathroom. I clean my teeth with John's French toothpaste and put a fingertip's spot of his aftershave on my wrist so I can have him with me all day.

On the ferry, Auntie Ruby is a bit down. Feathers has taken a fancy to the caravan next door and keeps going in there and annoying Auntie Vi. Auntie Vi says Feathers will end up covered in breadcrumbs and fried over a low simmer if she messes on Auntie Vi's patchwork quilt again. Auntie Vi is upset because there has been a revolution in the drying room.

Clem is also on the ferry. Now that professional fishermen from the mainland are trawling the kelp, he's only needed two days a week. He's going to the mall to look at the pet shop.

On the bus, I nod to Vince and he nods back. Jennifer nods too. They're starting to look like bookends. As I pass Justin and the Cools, Sophie shouts out, 'What's that stink of seaweed?' I reply, 'Must be your socks, Sophie, you haven't changed them for a week.' This is true but unkind. Now I'm Blanche, I think it's hugely funny.

Sophie just vibrates her head very quickly and says, 'Nuuur!'

The whole day at school is turned upside down with preparations for the concert. At lunchtime, Mr Thompson takes three Panadols and makes the Year Seven recorder band stay behind to straighten their chairs. They are truly pathetic. Half of them don't play at all. They just stand there holding their recorders five centimetres away from their mouths and wiggling their fingers vaguely.

After school I don't bother to go home. I curl up at the back of the hall with a book from the public library. It's called *Traps and Tips for the Small Businessman*. It has a man called Joe Smith as an example of how not to do things.

Joe Smith's life is a series of disasters and he is almost bankrupted about thirty-five times. He is a total moron. He reminds me of Herr Schulz in our German book. Herr Schulz is always losing things and forgetting what shopping he set out for and missing his bus to the sports club. Joe Smith's wife Joan reminds me of Frau Schulz, too. They both seem to spend their lives cheerfully getting their idiot husbands out of trouble and feeding them huge

214

dinners. Joan Smith knows a lot about tax loopholes. Heidi Schulz is very big on apple strudel. Personally, I'd get a divorce.

My Social Studies teacher, Mrs Mills, is doing the make-up. She gives me a completely white face with crimson lips. My eyeballs look yellow.

The concert has started. I look out of a hole in the curtains. The Principal is rabbiting on. I can see Blanche, Clem, Col, George and Stella. No John. The band does its medley. Still no John. The Year Seven recorder band goes on, then the Year Eleven dance troupe.

They do a routine called 'Pumpin''. It's amazingly energetic and involves very revealing lycra costumes. There is only one boy in it, and he's running with sweat because he has to throw each girl about and still keep smiling.

Lies goes on. They are taking so long to get their sound system organised that Miss Simpson goes up on the stage and gets some old crone to draw the raffle tickets. Miss Simpson is wearing a very short black cocktail dress with dangly gold earrings. She also seems to be looking around for John.

Lies belts out 'Lover' at a million

decibels. Kylie shouts 'Ya suck!' a few times at the treasurer of the P&C. There's a polite splatter of applause.

It's interval and he's still not there. I get depressed. I sniff my wrist but there's no smell left. The time ticks on. It's time for us. Ben Traversi switches on the tape deck. It starts to hiss. The music blasts out.

Jennifer walks on dramatically in her gorgeous lacy nightie from the theatrical costume place. She looks around with mad, jerky movements and says, 'My heart is heavy tonight. It must be the melancholy call of the West Wind. The Wild West Wind. The Bleak West Wind ...' This is the cue for the Spirits of the West Wind to start wailing and entering from the left flapping their arms.

It's at this point that Dylan comes up behind me and puts his hand over my mouth. I have a big handprint in my white make-up. Mrs Mills has to do an emergency job on me. I miss the first wailing section. I sneak onto the stage as Jennifer is falling in love with the Spirit of Change (which is Vince without his mask). My family all wave. I scan the audience for John. He's not there. Vince is supposed to look sophisticated. He looks a complete dork. He wears George's hat and suit and a pair of sunglasses.

I suddenly see John. My stomach does a backflip. He's making his way across the seats at the back. He grins and does a thumbs-up. But he doesn't sit down. He's making his way towards a group of teachers. He's making his way towards Miss Simpson! I'm stunned. The Spirits of the West Wind have to sway. I sway, but I'm staring at John. He goes right up to Miss Simpson. He takes her by the arm! She's as astonished as I am. She gets very sparkly and leggy and keeps looking over her shoulders at the other teachers.

I can't believe this! He leads her to the back of the hall. He starts talking earnestly to her. I know he's desperate because Babette's dumped him, but you'd think he could wait until after the concert! The Spirits of the West Wind have to wail. I wail. I'm fuming. Fortunately, it's time for Cordelia's ballet so I just have to stand around. What are they talking about? It's time for the human screwdriver. I snatch onto Cordelia's leg and start walking in a circle. My back is to the audience. I keep sneaking looks over my shoulder but for a few tense seconds my view's obscured. As I finish the turn, I'm stunned. He's leading her away by the arm!

We go into the second turn. But I don't. I forget. I'm staring at John and Miss Simpson. She's touching him on the arm. Get your hands off him! Cordelia starts to hop to keep her balance. She hisses, 'Move!' I guiltily move, but it's too fast, too late. Now Cordelia is doing frantic little hops on the spot and the other two Spirits of the West Wind are swearing at me. We cling to the leg. Cordelia hops off with the three of us attached. In desperation she suddenly bursts free. She improvises a few high leaps and spins about the stage.

She collides with Vince, who's walking on backwards. Vince spins round early. Three kids in the audience start bellowing in horror at his Freddy Krueger mask. They bawl all the way through Jennifer's appeal to death. The audience is straining to hear what Jennifer is saying. Jennifer is supposed to whisper, 'With my last, faint breath I beg you ... remember the rainforest.' Instead, she ends up bellowing it out like a football fan at the Grand

Final. For someone at death's door she's got the best lungs.

When Cordelia takes her bow, it's obvious she's been crying. Jennifer is also crying. Vince hisses at me, 'You did that deliberately.'

I don't care what they all think. I have to find John. I run out the back of the hall. I'm still in my make-up and costume. I clutch my veil. There's no sign of John or Miss Simpson. Then I see them. They're under the big light by the basketball courts. They're in a clinch! Are they? No. I'm hopeless without my glasses. I squint. Miss Simpson is reading something. John is standing very close to her, reading over her shoulder.

Blow this. I won't give them time to get into a clinch. I run towards them. The gravel digs into my bare feet. John sees me. His face is alive with delight.

'Em, the most amazing thing! I finally managed to get through to Yarradindi Beers. They've gone bust, they can't pay us.'

'How can that be good news?'

John laughs with delight.

'It's not good news. It's terrifying news. It means we're owed a fortune and we now have nobody to buy our kelp. But Em, ten minutes after that call I got a fax from Japan! The Japanese want to buy up the island!'

Chapter 30

I just stand there.

'And here's a bonus for you, Em. You know that school you want to go to? I've got you in. Next term.'

John goes on to explain how the Japanese company plan to build a huge new seaweed processing factory at North Beach, where their large boats can moor in safety. It will be like the one that John had planned but much bigger. It will have special concrete tanks for growing Bobbly Brains so it can be monitored and harvested easily. Inside, it will have fully automated drying rooms. It will employ two Japanese technicians and three locals. Local deep-sea fishermen will harvest the bull kelp in huge loads from the open sea. The wildlife will continue to be protected.

All Tates will be given a large sum of money to leave the island. We will also receive a yearly fee and we will all be given new houses on the mainland.

The island will become an eco-resort. Our house will be turned into a hotel with a staff from the mainland. A new, 200-seat ferry will run from the mainland. A swimming pool will be put in and the caravan park will be made part of a golf course.

Just then, Blanche, Clem and Col come out to find me and I tell them the news.

There is, as they say, a scene. Blanche hits the roof. When George and Stella appear with Vince, Blanche turns on George. Which is a bit unfair, since it's the first George has heard about it, too. All the people leaving the concert stare. Blanche screams at John, 'How dare you sell out our livelihood!'

'You haven't got a livelihood anymore!' John replies.

'We'll just sell to somebody else!'

'There isn't another company that buys kelp in this form! We'd have to re-equip completely.'

'Oh rubbish!'

John looks absolutely ferocious. And I

can't understand how I could have thought Blanche was mellowing.

'Don't you think I've tried to find another buyer? I've been warning you about Yarradindi Beers from the minute I set foot on the island! If you and your father hadn't been so dense this never would have happened!'

John starts to go. Blanche yells at him. 'You might persuade Emily to side with you, but there's no way Tiff will!'

John stops and stares at Blanche. 'Actually, she's already agreed.'

The journey back on the ferry is historic. John stands at the front, staring out to sea. Blanche stands at the back staring out to sea. Clem and I sit inside, huddled together. Clem doesn't say anything but he keeps shifting position. I think he's terrified at the thought of leaving the island.

As we're leaving the ferry, Blanche says to me, 'Do you honestly want to sell the island?' I realise that I don't want to sell the island. I realise I really care about the island, but John is saying it's the right thing to do. I don't know what I want.

Blanche powers up to the house to confront Tiff. But Rod opens the door. He's all twinkly and awkward. Tiff, equally twinkly, comes up and links her arm through his huge, furry elbow. She bursts out, 'We're engaged! And we're getting a new house in the Ocean Meadows development with my share of the money, so the children will be closer to school! Oh Blanche, isn't it wonderful!'

Tiff beams and I see the glint of her first gold tooth.

I'm inclined to think it *is* wonderful. She wanted her man and she got him. But Blanche does not agree. In fact, Blanche thinks it's treachery, and storms at poor Tiff until Tiff visibly wilts under the verbal barrage and turns pathetically to me.

'Look, Em, you decide. I'll vote with you.' And she hurries off with Rod.

Blanche says, 'I hope you realise what you're doing.' She strides off, fuming.

John turns to me. 'Well, Em, it looks as if it's up to you.'

I feel weird. This used to be what I dreamed of—the fate of the island in my hands, an international deal, a huge fortune. Now I just want to run away.

I say desperately, 'Can't we start food processing on our own?'

'We could. If we could get a partner to invest the money for development and marketing. But that could take years. And it could be years before you started to see a return on your money. And what would you all live on in the meantime? If we could have got the cosmetics side going we might have had a chance. But, there you go . . .'

My stomach is full of butterflies.

'But Col and Clem, without the factory, I'm afraid they'll . . .'

What *am* I afraid of? Suddenly I know. I feel choked.

'I'm . . . I'm afraid they'll die.'

There's a silence and then John says softly, 'Look, you mustn't take all this from me. Get advice. See George. I'm sorry, Emily. This is business. Sometimes you have to know when to cut your losses and run.'

'Are you going to run?'

John gives a great laugh of bitter triumph.

'You're joking! I'm seeing this deal through! They won't rip me off like they did your grandpa. I just wish I'd got here

earlier. I could have saved you the lot—
and made us all a fortune.'

He's grimly excited. He's like Emily of
Emily Enterprises about to go into battle.
Except that Emily of Emily Enterprises
was just a stupid daydream.

'When do I have to decide?'

'As soon as possible.'

I go for a walk on the beach. The
factory is lit up with lights like fairy land.
Fatty whimpers at me from behind the seal
fence.

I'm so lost in thought that at first I
don't notice them. The family. They come
in twos and threes. They come in little
boats. They assemble on the beach about
twenty metres away, just watching. The
word has got around. They are waiting for
my decision. Then, one by one, they slowly
walk away and leave me to my thoughts.

I sit on the sand and hug my knees. I
pretend Grandpa has never died. I pretend
the only thing I have to worry about is
fielding insults between Grandpa and
Blanche.

It's getting cold. Clem and Col come
and sit next to me, one on either side.
They don't say anything. They're like two
big rocks. It's nice.

Then Col coughs and says, 'Emily. Clem and me ... well, we reckon John knows what he's doing.'

Clem adds, 'And we reckon you should go to that school, Em. Because you're a clever girl, and you should have a good education.'

I feel tears. I ask, 'But what about you?'

There's a silence and then Clem says, 'Being honest, Emmy, nowadays we don't do much here anyhow.'

It's true and it breaks my heart. Col and Clem are gazing out to sea. I look at the sticky tape on the hinge of Col's glasses. I search for something to say.

'There's a really good competition on the packet of our detergent pack. You win a holiday in Las Vegas.'

Clem doesn't say anything. Col gives a tight little smile. He pushes his glasses back up his nose and says, 'We can afford our own holidays, now.'

I sit on the beach a long time. Tomorrow I will go to George, just to keep John happy. But I know what I am going to do. I am going to sell the island.

Chapter 31

Blanche storms and raves. When she says
to me, 'I warned you he'd take away the
island!', I want to die. But it's the right
decision. Miss Simpson helps John send
off a fax to the Japanese company. I have
a nightmare where the ferry sinks and
everyone drowns.

Now that I'm excluded from the Cools
I'm mostly alone at school. Dylan Pocky
and Kylie have become an item. I try to daydream but I don't feel like it much any more.
Emily Enterprises seems plain silly.

One day I'm sitting outside the Science
Block eating my lunch and half-heartedly
trying to read the *Financial Review* when
Vince comes up. He sits in silence for a
while and then he shoves his glasses back
up his nose.

'For what it's worth, I think you're doing the right thing. And I think John is right.' Weirdly, I feel tears come to my eyes. I swallow them down because I'm not sure whether he's being sarcastic. I sneak a look at him. He's not. I say, 'Thanks.'

I see Jennifer hovering in the background. Vince gets up. He says, 'Anyhow, I just wanted to say, you know, I'm sorry.'

I look at him. He's changed. He's taller, maybe, more confident. Maybe it's just that he's with Jennifer.

'That's okay,' I say. 'And I'm sorry I stuffed up at the concert.' Vince shrugs. 'To tell you the truth,' he looks around guiltily and gives a little conspiratorial grin, 'Don't tell Jen, but I felt like a complete geek.'

Jen. Yes. It's being with her that's done it. He moves off. He puts his arm around Jennifer's shoulders and she slips an arm around his waist. They're easy together. Complete. Grown-up. Meanwhile I'm still at about the emotional age of ten. With a crush on someone who hardly knows I exist.

I am pathetic. That night I go straight to my room. I avoid John.

Tiff and the kids move out to a place on the mainland. Their dream home in Ocean Meadows will be completed in two months. Work at the factory goes on, but largely in silence. Clem gets the flu. He has to spend a week in bed.

Ms Emily Tate
Tate Island
Victoria
Australia

Dear Miss Tate,

Mr Murdoch thanks you for your kind letter and wishes you every success in your chosen career.

Yours sincerely,

F W Paterson

For and on behalf of
Rupert Murdoch

Blanche, Mrs Lee and I go and look at a display home in the Ocean Meadows estate. From the bus, I always admired the Ocean Meadows houses. They have neat, identical gardens. They have clean, fawn bricks. But when we go inside one I feel odd. It's white and gleaming. It has cane furniture and curtains with a pattern of tropical flowers. I feel as if I'm walking through the pages of one of the women's magazines in Rod's waiting room.

I try to imagine the walls covered with portraits of Tates. I try to imagine Feathers living in the built-in wardrobes.

Mrs Lee doesn't like the house at all. She disapproves of all the windows. She says it's an easy target. She says the first thing we'd have to do is fill the spa bath with rolled up balls of alfoil.

School drags on. Yarradindi Beers closes down. Every time I pass a Yarradindi Doug poster I feel a bit sad. John's working from morning till night in the office. Miss Simpson comes over after school to do translations. I hurry home to run errands for John. One day I get back and men wearing hard helmets are walking all over North Beach with tape measures and gadgets on tripods.

A man from an architect's office arrives with five large cardboard boxes. I help him unpack them. They contain layers and layers of packaging. It is a model of the new factory and resort. It has little people and trees and a blue plaster of Paris sea. There are tiny seals.

On the morning that the Japanese are coming for a final inspection I wake up to brilliant sunshine. Blanche has to go to work. Before she leaves, she blinks a lot at me and says in a weird, husky voice, 'We'll get it back, you know. We *will* get it back.'

The delegation is due at 11.00 am. John has gone to fetch them in the launch. Miss Simpson will be translating. Auntie Ruby is keeping the ferry at the mainland because it isn't posh enough.

Vince and I go to North Beach for a last look. Fatty capers alongside. We stand and look out to sea. We both get a bit teary. Vince puts his arm around me.

'Well,' he says, 'whoever owns the island on paper, it still really belongs to us.'

When we get back to South Beach, they still haven't arrived. We wait and wait. Tiff joins us. Col and Clem are waiting too. Then Clem gets very anxious. He says he's going to watch TV in the van. Col goes with him.

I realise that both of them have started to walk with a stoop.

Finally, John's launch appears on the horizon. It moors at the jetty. The whole family gathers in silence. John motions ashore four Japanese businessmen and a female translator. Miss Simpson gets off behind them with George.

They bow and smile and admire everything. They look at samples of the kelp. It turns out that John has already taken them up to North Beach. All that they need to do now is to look at the model and sign the documents. We go into the factory where the model has been set up. The documents will be signed in the office by the Japanese businessmen, John, Tiff and me.

Vince and I stand by the door as John shows off the model. They all admire it. One of them picks up a model seal and says something. They all laugh. One passes around a packet of cigarettes. They all light up. I feel someone watching me. I look over my shoulder and see Col and Clem in the distance, peering towards the plant.

It's then that I hear the ferry hooting. It's hooting nonstop and plunging along at top speed. On the deck is Nanny Ethel and an army of little old Aboriginal ladies in floral dresses. They are all shaking their fists.

Before the ferry's even properly stopped, Nanny Ethel and another woman are hurling the gangplank over the side. Nanny pounds up the jetty. She has her stockwhip under her arm.

'Never in my born days!' she shouts. 'A factory on North Beach! You thieves! You miserable heap of possum poop! Come out and show your faces!'

She cracks her stockwhip. (If you haven't heard a stockwhip crack you should know that it sounds like a gunshot.) The Japanese freeze.

Nanny bellows, 'Get out here!' The Japanese consult their interpreter. Miss Simpson adds a few words.

The party of Japanese comes out, foll-owed by John, George, Tiff and Miss Simpson. Their eyebrows shoot up. They're looking at a sea of spectacles. At the front are about fifty elderly Aboriginal women with folded arms and murderous stares. At the front of these is Nanny Ethel with her stockwhip under her arm.

Shocked, all the businessmen raise

their cigarettes to their lips. But Nanny Ethel's stockwhip is snaking through the air, cracking and whistling. Crack, crack, crack! It flips past their faces. It cracks around their feet. On the ground in front of the Japanese businessmen are a pile of cigarette ends. Sticking out of their mouths are just the filter tips.

The crowd gasps. Nanny winds up her stockwhip casually. 'And I'd thank you gentlemen not to smoke.'

Chapter 32

Nanny stands on a chair so everyone can see her.

'This island is sacred to my people.' She lets the Japanese lady translate. The Japanese businessmen are looking really worried. 'I and some of these ladies are its special keepers. North Beach was never built on because it has secret caves with special paintings which only women are allowed to see. The man known as Great-Great-Grandpa Tate was allowed to build on this island only on condition he stuck to the South.'

Nanny goes on to say that she will take a party of women to see the caves as proof. She says she will go to the highest court in the land to save Tate Island. She also implies she will get pretty dangerous with her whip.

Everyone goes off to North Beach. Nanny and the ladies lead in the ferry with Vince and me. John, Tiff, Miss Simpson, George and the Japanese follow in the launch. Behind them come dozens of little boats bearing Tates. On the launch Vince asks Nanny why she never told him about the island. She gives him a withering look and says it's women's business and nothing to do with him. Not even George knows. If Nanny hadn't been up at the rodeos, she says, she would have nipped this whole darn nonsense in the bud.

At North Beach, the crowd peels back for Nanny as if she's the Queen. I suppose she is, really. Nanny says she will show the cave paintings, but only to women. She calls Miss Simpson and the Japanese lady interpreter. Then she turns to me, 'And you, Emily. It's about time you learnt a bit about this island.'

The Japanese interpreter tells her boss what she's doing. He and his mates have a talk about it. They're looking really rattled.

Nanny warns that no-one else is to follow. She sets off into the bush. I follow with Miss Simpson and the Japanese lady. Miss Simpson ladders her tights after about two seconds. We slog on through the bush. Nanny stops us next to some huge, towering rocks. She tells us to wait. She disappears through a slit in the rock.

Bush flies buzz around our faces. Miss Simpson and I smile politely at the Japanese lady. She smiles politely back. I bet she wishes she hadn't landed this job. There's a difficult silence. Miss Simpson starts talking in Japanese. She explains to me that she is telling the Japanese lady about her trip to Tokyo with the Secondary School Teachers' Language Association. The Japanese lady nods and smiles between swatting flies.

Nanny finally emerges. We follow her into a cave. At first it is too dark to see anything. Then, as our eyes get accustomed to the gloom, we see these amazing cave paintings. There are dolphins, fish, kangaroos, albatross and seals.

And then, we see it. It is a painting of an old sailing boat with two huge masts. It's in full sail. It looks like a pirate ship. Nanny nods to me and says, 'That's your Great-Great-Grandpa's boat, Emily.'

The Japanese lady gasps. In a corner is a figure of a man. His hair comes out from his head in a big, reddish halo. In his hand is a seal harpoon. I gasp.

Because on his face is a pair of huge, round glasses.

He is unmistakable. He's been staring down at me from the hall all my life. 'But that's . . . that's . . .' I stammer.

'Yep, that's him. That's your Great-Great Grandpa. My mum used to tell me about him. She reckoned he couldn't use a spear to save his life. Our blokes used to be in fits.'

The Japanese can't get off the island quickly enough. Everyone cheers as John drives them off in the launch. The rest of the crowd finds itself back outside the factory. We're hugging each other. We're laughing and talking. Nanny does a display with her whip.

'Watch this!' Clem suddenly shouts.

With one mighty wrench, he rips out a section of the seal fence. The seals come galloping through, barking. We all cheer again. Col starts singing 'For She's a Jolly Good Fellow' to Nanny Ethel. Then we all sing 'For WE are Jolly Good Fellows'.

It becomes a party. If we Tates have not been good at parties in the past, we are learning now. Blanche arrives back in the middle of it all. She stands on the jetty and gives a speech about how the island will never leave the Tates and the Tates will never leave the island. We all cheer. John's launch docks at the jetty and Blanche, expansive with victory, beckons him ashore with a theatrical wave.

'Welcome home, John! You see, those new-fangled ideas of yours were no good for Tate Island . . .'

'Three cheers for John!'

It's Clem, of course. And of course we cheer. But John's pale. He stares around at the sea of spectacles.

'Blanche, it's obvious that you and the rest of the family want to keep the island. I respect that. But we are in very serious financial trouble here . . .'

'Garbage!' says Blanche. 'We've been in serious financial trouble for as long as I can remember. We always came through. Have a piece of Mrs Lee's cake . . .'

I find myself with Nanny, talking about the cave paintings.

'The most amazing thing was that painting of Great-Great-Grandpa Tate. The way he had those glasses.'

Nanny's mouth twitches. She says, 'Yeah,' and looks away.

'Nanny . . .!'

She packs up laughing. She's rolling around.

'Your faces! It was only the glasses! I swear, Em! The animals and the ship and the old fella have been there as long as anyone can remember! It was only the glasses!'

I'm shocked. So's Stella.

'Mum, how could you tamper with something like that . . .!'

'It's only chalk! Anyhow, I was fighting for the island. And remember. I'm a Tate. And you know what they say about Tates.'

Nanny's friends all shout, 'Never trust a Tate', and hoot with laughter. They laugh so much that their glasses steam up. They are, of course, all Tates.

Stella sighs and shakes her head. She reckons it's desecration. But I'm with Nanny. Whatever supernatural being is in charge of Tate Island, it's clearly got a sense of humour.

I get roped into a jiving competition by Nanny's friends. Then I have to play with the kids. Then I have to help Mrs Lee with the washing up. By the time I'm free to see John it's late and he's gone to bed. He's hardly slept for weeks organising this deal.

I walk along the beach, past the seals. It's lovely to see them home again. At the back of my mind there is the nagging worry about the future of the island. If only we could turn the kelp into moisturiser! And have everybody turn dark green. That's Tate Island for you. Gives with one hand and takes away with the other. Oh well. We'll think of something. *John and I* will think of something.

I go to bed happy for the first time in weeks. Next morning I sleep in. I stagger into the kitchen. Mrs Lee is singing Rolling Stones hits. There is an envelope next to my plate. It's in John's handwriting.

Dear Emily,

You were right! The Tates need this island, and they will always find a way to keep it! I'm leaving, Em, because I don't think my way of doing things is workable for your family. I've put the details in a letter to George, but you should know that I've given all but two per cent of my share of the business to you. I'm keeping that two per cent because I know you will make a fortune out of that blasted kelp and I want some of the action!

Forgive me for leaving without saying goodbye. I have to catch a plane. I'll write. You do too!

Good luck.

Love,

John.

Chapter 33

There is a hole in the pit of my stomach.

'Mrs Lee, when did John leave this?'

'Oh, I'm not sure. Ten minutes ago?'

I'm out of the house. I'm running towards the jetty. A large, smooth stone is rising in my throat. He's gone! He's gone!

He's on the jetty. He's got his suitcase and his jacket and hat. The ferry is coming over the horizon.

'John!'

I run up to him. I'm out of breath. I don't know what to say.

'Hello, Em!' He's awkward. 'I didn't expect you up so early!'

I just stand there. I realise that he was deliberately leaving before I woke up. His image glistens and goes jagged through my tears.

I don't mean to, but suddenly I'm clinging to him.

'Don't go! Please!'

'Hey, Em . . .'

He's anxious. He's got his arms around me. His chest is warm and hard and smells of cotton. There's a thread coming off one of the buttons on his blue shirt. It's like my dream. We're on the jetty and he's holding me. But now it's a nightmare. He gently untangles me and holds me by the elbows.

'Emily . . .'

He's looking at me.

'Try to understand. There's nothing here for me now.'

'There's *me*!'

How can I not count? How can I love him so much and he not care about me? I think of Justin. And Babette.

I take a deep breath and ask, 'Are you going back to Babette?'

'If she'll have me.'

Don't cry, you can do that later. Remember everything that's happening. His loose shirt button. The mole on his neck.

The ferry comes closer. He's looking down at me, worried. Memories flash past me. John at the airport . . . John at the dance . . .

'Em, I've got to go. Look . . .'

I can't help it. I burst out, 'But I love you!' and the stone in my throat fills it and aches.

He's silent for a moment and then he says softly, 'I know. And I'm very flattered, but I'm in love with somebody else.'

The ferry is about to dock. I'm numb.

'Oh Em, you don't want an old guy like me! You need someone your own age. And there will be someone!'

Sure, John.

'You're smart, you're attractive! And you've got a *fantastic* business mind! Some young chap out there won't know what hit him!'

I've lost him. He's here in my arms but he's really on the plane. He's in Europe. With her.

And I'm not here either. I'm staring at his shirt button but I'm on a hill. It's rising up beneath me and I can't stop it or even move. I'm going higher, so high that all I can see are tiny people and blue sea and little dots for seals. And when the hill gets high enough, it will curve over like a wave and I'll fall. I'll fall crashing, spinning, down. Into such terrible pain that I can't imagine. That is what will happen.

The ferry is here. He kisses me on the forehead. I can feel exactly where it is. It's like a brand.

'I'll write. You must write too. Let me know what's going on.'

We look at each other. He says softly, 'Bye, Em.'

The stone in my throat swells and turns over.

'Goodbye.'

I watch him get on the ferry. He doesn't look back. I try to remember everything. He goes inside the ferry and sits down. I can just see him. He puts on his sunglasses. He pushes them back up his nose, just like a Tate.

I'm in love with somebody else.

Every time his image glistens and gets jagged, I wipe my eyes. The ferry moves off. I watch until it gets to the mainland. The kiss is imprinted on my forehead. It still tingles. The stone has grown downwards to fill my chest. I take off my glasses because they are wet with tears.

So this is despair.

I don't fall from the mountain. I'm just suspended in an empty, silent space. And

I don't dream of John, although I try to. I want to dream of him because it's getting harder to remember his face. Which is weird, because I can remember his shirt button and the mole on his neck as vividly as a photograph.

Sometimes I do remember his face. It's when I'm not thinking about him. He'll flash up, dazzlingly clear. He's always smiling. He's usually on the beach. I get a flash of happiness and then the stone moves up into my throat. Normally the stone sits in my chest. It grazes when I breathe.

Jean-Paul Tate-Coteau. I write his name a lot. I miss him absolutely. I see him on every corner. He left his toothpaste so I keep it in my second drawer.

The family has serious money problems. I haven't got the heart to take part in the business—not that there is any business to run. The factory stands silent. Blanche and George keep advertising for investors to help us set up the food-processing plant. But the two that reply want to run the whole thing themselves. We are all living on our savings. Rod gives us some money.

Blanche keeps working at the Supa Market. The aunties and Clem and Col get a bit of work fruit-picking for two weeks on the mainland. I get a job delivering junk mail after school.

John sends me picture postcards from France. In one he mentions that he and Babette are together again. I write him long, despairing love letters. I tear them up. I send postcards of Australian wildlife. I stick to school and the weather.

Miss Simpson misses him too. Her skirts get longer and she doesn't laugh as much. I go off her one lunchtime when I see her in the shopping mall. She's with Mr Taylor, the Design and Technology teacher. They're definitely flirting.

One day I'm with Nanny Ethel. Her tales of life on the trail are amazing. They stop me thinking of John. We're in her room. She wears her battered Akubra hat as usual when she's relaxing. She's polishing one of her saddles with some homemade green gunk. She tells me about the time her best mate got bitten by a snake in a flash flood. She had to get him and their horses and cattle across the river to safety.

She gives me a Mintie. We're both chewing. She says suddenly, 'You still moping about that bald Pom?'

'He is not bald.'

'Give him ten years. He'll be bald as a billiard ball. Them dark Tates all end up baldies.'

She swings the saddle back up on its hook. Her hands are covered in green gunk. She looks at herself in the mirror. She starts rubbing the green gunk all over her face.

'Nanny!'

'There's kelp in that. Brings your skin up beautiful, kelp.'

'Right. If you want to turn green.'

'Kelp doesn't turn you green. Not if you wipe it off with bush honey and banksia root.'

I stare at Nanny.

Chapter 34

My first instinct is to run and tell George and Blanche. But then I realise that they're so panicked about money they'd fob off the whole idea as a kid's daydream. I have to show them facts and figures. I go to the office and get the scientist's report out of its file. My hands are shaking.

The kelp needs to be packed in airtight, glass jars. I get out the *Yellow Pages*. I put on my deepest voice. I find out the cost of glass jars, labels and boxes. I locate a second-hand machine that seals glass jars. I find out how much it is to advertise in local papers and health magazines. I rack my brains for everything John ever taught me. By 12.30 am I've typed a report.

The next night, Tiff and Rod give a

dinner for Vince and his parents and Blanche and me. We all get a hard slab of lasagna. It tastes like tennis shoe and tomato sauce. Halfway through, Tiff says nervously, 'I got a call from the bank today. They want us to sell off part of the island for holiday homes.'

My heart starts pounding.

'No way,' says Blanche. 'We'll re-advertise for investors.'

'Blanche,' George says, 'we don't have a choice.'

I cough. My voice comes out all high and strangled. I say, 'Actually, we do.'

I get out the documents. I talk my way through them. I explain we need $10,000 for costs and advertising. I argue that if we do lose that, it will be covered by the cost of the land sale we'll have to make anyway. Every time somebody tries to interrupt, I plough on. I avoid Blanche's eye. As I get to the end, I realise they are all looking at me in amazement. George and Tiff turn instinctively to Blanche. Blanche is frowning, dumbstruck.

There's a silence.

Blanche blinks. She opens her mouth

then closes it. She stares at me with this odd look of surprise. She says, 'Well. We can only give it a try . . .'

Our face pack comes in two sizes. We also sell a leather cleaner. It's made of exactly the same ingredients as the face pack, but we don't let on. Vince designs Aboriginal art labels. Our brand name is 'Dolphin Dreaming'. Nanny wanted her photo on it but she was outvoted.

Everyone in the family is working again. The vats are churning away just like in the old days. An army of uncles and aunties spoon the kelp into the jars. Everyone wears lab coats. With each little jar of kelp we provide a matching jar of bush honey and mashed-up banksia root gathered by Nanny and her friends.

I persuade Blanche to put a big ad in a city newspaper. It's a gamble. We borrow more money from Rod. The ad describes Nanny's green gunk as an ancient Aboriginal remedy shrouded in mystery. We put in the bit from the scientific report that says our kelp mixture is as good for the skin as all the pricey stuff from Europe. It doesn't say that Nanny also uses it on her saddles.

We sweat blood for two days. Then

the mail orders start coming and coming! Soon they're coming like crazy! The most exciting thing is when a big daily paper does an article on us. Nanny steals the limelight by posing with her stockwhip and looking mystical. She goes on a talk show and enquiries flood in.

Blanche and I get an appointment with a company that runs a chain of chemist shops in Sydney. We have to go by plane! All the way there, Blanche nags me about how she's going to run the interview and I'm to shut up. I'm close to strangling her. As we get outside the appointment room, she suddenly insists on finding a toilet. We hurry into their posh dunnies. Blanche sinks down on a chair. I'm fuming because we'll be late. I wait for her to lecture me about something or other. But she just stares at the wall.

I suddenly realise that she is terrified.

She whispers, 'It's no good . . . Em, can you go in on your own?'

I could, but they'd never listen to me, I need Blanche! And I realise that for once, Blanche needs me!

I have to get her in there, even if she doesn't open her mouth. I beg. I plead. Finally, I say casually, 'Well, John would laugh if he saw us now, wouldn't he . . .?'

Blanche stirs and gives a throaty growl. I quickly drag her to her feet. With my arm under her elbow, we shuffle off towards the door.

Blanche spends the whole meeting staring at the wall in blank, stony terror. I make the sale. Afterwards, of course, she doesn't mention a word about being frightened. That's Blanche. But on the journey back, I catch her looking at me. She has an odd light in her eye. Admiration? Blanche?

She smiles at me. I smile back.

Chapter 35

Now the orders are swamping us. We have to use a handcart to bring our sacks of mail-order forms from the ferry to the house. Martin comes back from the mainland to do the job. He puts the sacks in the kitchen. Mrs Lee sprinkles them with nutmeg to confuse the aliens.

I write and tell John. By return mail comes the most beautiful leather briefcase with my initials in gold. There is a note saying, 'Told you so! Love John'. I take it to the end of the beach to hug. I try not to get tears on the leather.

Gradually, we are buying ourselves out of our debts. Everyone on the island is happy. The aunties have worked out their pecking order. Feathers has her own luxurious, carpeted cage. Inspired by his trip on the feral tractor, Col has bought himself a go-kart. I get to chuck away my plate because Rod says my bite has straightened.

As for Rod, he, Tiff and the kids are blissfully happy in their new house. None of the children has fillings, but Tiff has a mouth full of pure gold. Tiff and Rod take Clem with them to get a dog from the pound. They end up with two dogs called Prince and Princess. Clem visits them daily. Rod cleans their teeth with dental floss. They have a special doggy toothbrush.

Mrs Lee is staying with us. She has made a new woman of Blanche. Mrs Lee says she has never felt more at home than on the island. This figures since everybody else on the island is also completely mad. She cooks and cleans like an angel. She never takes holidays. That's not counting two weeks in November. This is when she is taken into the mothership. The aliens put probes into her brain. They want vital information about the army. They also want her recipe for chicken stockpot.

Blanche rapidly gains confidence at business meetings. In fact, for a while I regret that I encouraged her. But then I realise something. I realise that Blanche is really a combination of Joe Smith from *Tips and Traps for Small Businessmen* and Herr Schulz from our German book. Because she's short-sighted, all I have to do to handle her is behave like Joan Smith and read any small print. With Mrs Lee providing the dinners, it's a breeze. Blanche is on top of the world of course, because, like Joe Smith, she assumes all the ideas are hers.

There were a frightening few days when Blanche went stockcar racing with Terry Pocky. He had come into the Supa Market to get a bottle of Pepsi and a packet of CocoPops for his breakfast. They made a truce over the cheese. I was worried. I don't think I could cope with Dylan Pocky as my brother. But, thank heavens, it seems to have fizzled out.

And there's the most incredible thing. Well, two incredible things. Blanche and I go to Sydney for a meeting with an international fashion store. I take my briefcase and I stand straight and emit confidence. Although Blanche is starting to become Joe Smith, I outmanoeuvre her by doing Joan Smith combined with John plus a bit of Sophie from school. It goes brilliantly.

When we come out, Blanche takes my arm.

Now this is the amazing bit. We come out into the sunshine and we're standing at the lights. A big, chauffeur-driven black car is idling right in front of us waiting to turn left. The window is down and I can see the man in the back quite clearly. He is reading some papers. He puts them down.

It is Mr Murdoch!

I jump up and down and shout, 'It's me! Mr Murdoch! It's Emily!'

He looks a bit alarmed. As the car pulls off I start running alongside.

'You'll never guess! The kelp! We're selling it as a face pack! We're going international!'

I'm pounding alongside the car.

He looks at me, bewildered and says, 'That's wonderful, dear, I . . .!'

I can't keep up. I stop and call out, 'If ever you're in the area! And thank you *so* much for all your letters!'

He's staring anxiously at me out of the back window. I wave, beaming. He waves back, sort of puzzled. My inspiration.

I'm still missing John, but it's not half as

painful. When I'm desperate I hug my briefcase. Which brings me to my second amazing thing.

I'm back in Yarradindi. Vince and I are at McDonald's. I've gone to his place after school to work on a new logo. As we're walking through the carpark, two people in McDonald's uniform come chasing after us. They have my briefcase. One is a dark-haired girl. The other is a guy.

He is tall and lanky with very blond hair and pimples. (Mind you, I always think a few pimples add character.)

I notice his name badge. It says 'Edmund'.

He stops, out of breath, and says, as they're trained to do, 'Ma'am!'

He holds out my briefcase.

'You left this.'

I have rehearsed this so many times it just comes out. I say, in this *incredibly* sexy voice, 'Thank you, Eddie. And please, my name is Emily.'

I gasp. I don't believe myself. How could I say that?

The girl snorts and hurries off to giggle next to the life-size Ronald McDonald. She is clearly not Conchita. But Eddie smiles cheekily. The paper hat's dumb, but he is *cute!* He flips his cloth over his arm.

He says, 'Okay. See you. *Emily.*'

Is this sarcasm? No, I think . . . I think he's interested!

As we walk through the carpark, Vince says, 'That's the new Year Ten guy. He's some kinda genius at Commerce.'

I look back. He's still standing there with his arms folded, staring. I feel this big, ridiculous giggle bubbling up. Well hi, Mr Commerce, prepare to meet your match!

His eyes are boring into my back. Vince and I stand at the traffic lights. A scruffy old seagull with one leg is perched on the cyclone fence. In the distance, Tate Island sparkles white and green in a turquoise ocean.

I am mistress of the universe and I think I have developed a sudden passion for Big Macs.

Is he still looking? *Yes!*

I smother a giggle. I stand straight and emit confidence. I chicken-wing like crazy all the way to the bus stop.

Linda Aronson
Rude Health

*'You're new, aren't you? With an odd name. Ian Grubby . . .
Snotty . . .' The whole class rocks with laughter. I swallow.
'Rude, sir. Ian Rude.'*

Ian Rude's whole life is embarrassment. With a name like
that, what can you expect? He's short. He's skinny. His
parents run a health food shop. Things really couldn't get
much worse – could they?

Then Ian discovers that he has secret superhuman powers –
and they land him in BIG trouble. Is he cursed? Is he a
genuine superkid? Or are the Teenage Energy Tablets (with
odourless garlic) his mum gives him stronger than she
realises?

A selected list of titles available from Macmillan and Pan Books

The prices shown below are correct at the time of going to press. However, Macmillan Publishers reserve the right to show new retail prices on covers which may differ from those previously advertised.

TIM WINTON

Lockie Leonard, Human Torpedo	0 330 34067 0	£3.99
Lockie Leonard, Scumbuster	0 330 34068 9	£3.99
Lockie Leonard, Legend	0 330 35496 5	£3.99

LINDA ARONSON

Rude Health	0 330 39060 0	£3.99

MORRIS GLEITZMAN

Two Weeks with the Queen	0 330 36749 0	£3.99
Blabber Mouth	0 330 33283 X	£3.99
Sticky Beak	0 330 33681 9	£3.99
Belly Flop	0 330 34522 2	£3.99
Water Wings	0 330 35014 5	£3.99

All Macmillan titles can be ordered at your local bookshop or are available by post from:

**Book Service by Post
PO Box 29, Douglas, Isle of Man IM99 1BQ**

Credit cards accepted. For details:
Telephone: 01624 675137
Fax: 01624 670923
E-mail: bookshop@enterprise.net

Free postage and packing in the UK.
Overseas customers: add £1 per book (paperback)
and £3 per book (hardback)